TO THE WALLS OF CARTAGENA

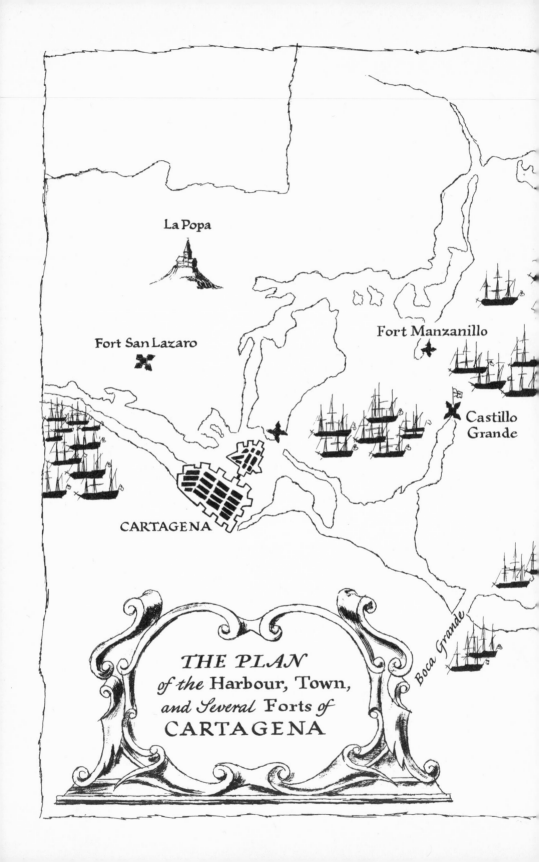

La Popa

Fort Manzanillo

Fort San Lazaro

Castillo Grande

CARTAGENA

Boca Grande

THE PLAN
of the Harbour, Town,
and Several Forts of
CARTAGENA

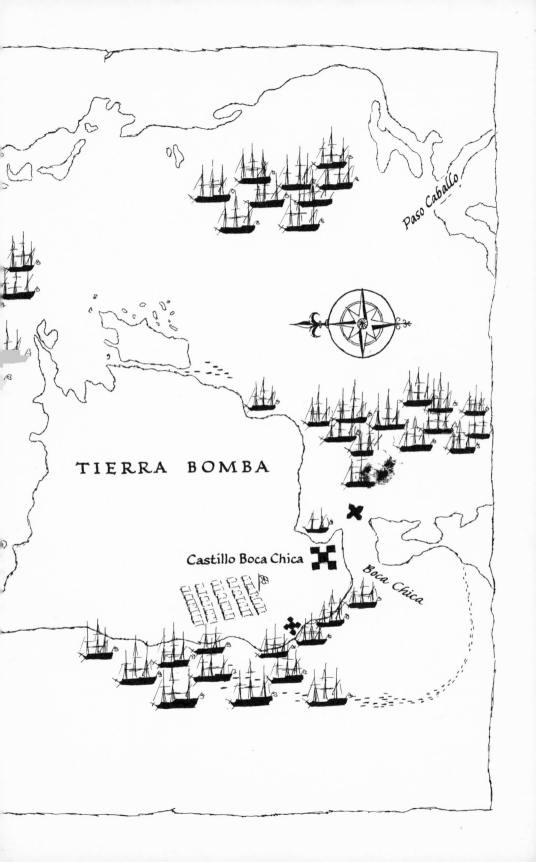

TO THE WALLS
OF CARTAGENA

By Allan Dwight

Illustrated by Leonard Vosburgh

COLONIAL WILLIAMSBURG

Williamsburg, Virginia

DISTRIBUTED BY

HOLT, RINEHART, AND WINSTON, INC.

New York

Contents

TO THE WALLS OF CARTAGENA

ONE

Public Times in Williamsburg

It was cool for late May, thought Greg Shelby as, with Rob Warren beside him, he started down the walk leading from the College of William and Mary to Duke of Gloucester Street. In the distance, at the far end of the broadest thoroughfare in the colony of Virginia, rose the massive brick Capitol topped by a graceful cupola from which now flew the flag of the Grand Union of Britain. A sudden breeze made Greg settle his cap more firmly on his head, for both he and Rob wore the customary cap and gown of students above grammar school grade at William and Mary.

Although it was now the short vacation between the end of the Easter term and the beginning of the Trinity term on June 2, most of the students, indeed all of them except those whose homes were near Williamsburg, had stayed at the college rather than undertake journeys to and from distant plantations.

As the two companions strolled past Bruton Parish Church they were joined by four other students who were also bound for the Capitol. Another session of the General Assembly of Virginia was being convened today by Lieutenant Governor William Gooch, representative of King George II in England. People were gathering along the street to see the Governor pass in his fine carriage on the way from his mansion, called the "Palace," to the Capitol for the ceremony.

A recent rain had laid the pale dust on the streets and washed clean the leaves of the shrubs and fruit trees and the gay flowers in the little gardens behind the white picket fences. It was exhilarating to be free of college routine on this bright morning in Williamsburg, thought Greg, but he also knew that he was lucky to be in the college which, he was sure, was as good as the Harvard College up in New England. He told himself again he must do well in his studies to justify the expense of an education his mother and father could scarcely afford.

By comparison with some colonial capitals, Williamsburg, in this year of 1740, was a small place. But to Greg, who, with the great majority of Virginians, lived in the country, it seemed a large and impressive town. It was true that for most of the year it had a quiet, placid air, but at important times such as this, or the convening of the General Court, it was bustling and crowded. Men who owned plantations, large or small, arrived with their attendants, bondservants or slaves, and often with their whole families. Wandering peddlers displayed their wares in Market Square or at the outdoor "Exchange" near the Capitol, and town merchants showed their newest goods from England.

Captains and sailors from ships in the James and York Rivers appeared on the streets and occasionally even an Indian from upcountry could be seen. Gentlemen pranced by on their best horses or escorted carriages filled with gaily dressed wives and daughters. Servants bustled importantly on errands between taverns, shops, and houses. Puppet shows were set up in Market Square, lawn bowling and wrestling matches were popular, while at the track just outside town planters raced their horses and bet heavily on their favorites. Nights were lively, with parties in homes and balls and gaming at cards and dice in taverns. Truly, Public Times brought color and excitement to Williamsburg.

Greg wished his mother and father could have come to the opening of the Assembly. But the small plantation of Pine Grove was a long day's ride on horseback or two or three days, depending on the weather, by jolting wagon. Coaches were becoming fashion-

able among a few wealthy planters, but their use was restricted by muddy roads or rivers that had to be ferried.

Market Square and the green around the powder magazine on the opposite side of the street were rimmed with wagons of farmers come to town with vegetables or chickens for sale. Here the crowds waiting to see the Governor were dense. As Greg and his friends reached the corner of Queen Street they heard the sound of a trumpet from the Palace.

"Let's go to the next corner," suggested Rob. "It's not so crowded there."

As they reached a clear spot on the sidewalk the Governor's coach turned the corner from Palace Green. Something squirmed against Greg's leg. Looking down he saw a small girl in a white pinafore, grasping some wilting pink roses, who was trying to push her way between him and Rob. Without a thought Greg swung her up on his shoulder as he would have his sister Susan, ignoring her gasped, "Oh, la!" By the time he had her firmly anchored and had removed a clutching hand from his ear, the finest coach in the colony, drawn by six spirited horses, its gilt shining, the Governor's coat of arms glowing on its doors, with liveried coachman and footman and a uniformed outrider, was almost upon them.

From the window Governor Gooch looked out benignly beneath the curls of his great wig, smiling and lifting his hand in response to the decorous clapping. He was an able and popular man, who, while doing his duty to the Crown, had insisted on changes in certain rules of the all-important tobacco trade with England which had benefitted the planters. Suddenly the child on Greg's shoulder threw her bouquet toward the coach. It fell short, but the gesture had caught the Governor's eye. He leaned forward and spoke to the coachman. The horses were pulled to a halt, the footman jumped down, picked up the bouquet and handed it to the Governor, who bowed and smiled his thanks to the child. The spectators cheered and clapped more loudly. The Governor rode on, holding the drooping roses.

"Ooooh," breathed the little girl happily.

The Governor's reputation for kindness and courtesy was well deserved, thought Greg.

"Come on," said Tom Norton, one of the students who had joined Greg. "We must make sure of getting into the House of Burgesses chamber when the Governor's speech is read there. We've come to hear what the King has to say to us."

"Dr. Blair will see to that," Rob told him confidently. "He wants us to watch our government at work, when we can."

Dr. Blair was a power in the colony second only to the Governor. Nearly fifty years earlier he had obtained the charter of the College of William and Mary in Virginia from Their Majesties William and Mary and had been its president ever since. He was also now the president of His Majesty's Council in Virginia, appointed by the Crown. This body had important functions in the government of the colony. In its legislative capacity it acted as an upper house of the General Assembly, the other being the House of Burgesses whose members were elected by the men of the counties. It was also, judicially, the highest court in the colony. And in an executive capacity it met with the Governor at times as an advisory body. A strong-willed Scots clergyman, Dr. Blair had sometimes differed with former governors and had not come off the worse for it, but now he seemed on amicable terms with Governor Gooch.

Greg set the little girl down gently, bowed to her curtsey and whispered "thank you," and hurried after the others.

At the Capitol the companions made their way through the growing throng on the grounds. As they passed through the arches of the entrance they saw the members of the House of Burgesses, led by their Speaker and walking two by two, leave the lower chamber and mount the stairs to the Council Chamber on the second floor where the Council awaited them. There, in joint session, they would hear the Governor's speech delivered. The boys were admitted to the Hall of the House of Burgesses by an usher who showed them to places along the wall where they could await the return of the members and the ceremony of reading the Governor's speech to the burgesses and privileged members of the public. After a half hour the burgesses returned, took their seats, and the Speaker read the speech to the assemblage and delivered it to the table where it was re-read sonorously by a clerk.

It was rather brief. It alluded indirectly to the war with Spain, which had been declared in the fall of the previous year, spoke flatteringly of His Majesty's concern for the protection of the colonies, and earnestly recommended the framing of a bill "to put our militia upon such a footing as will best enable them to contend with regular troops, who excel other men only by their exact discipline." At the end the audience applauded politely.

As they strolled back toward the college, Tom spoke of the Governor's careful references to the defense of the colony. "It's been known for two months that the British government has requested American troops to help an expedition against Spanish possessions in the Caribbean. They're already recruiting for it. Why didn't Governor Gooch come out plain about it? It's the first time England has ever asked for our help in a war overseas. We should be proud we're wanted."

"Maybe this is just the first step," suggested one boy. "He's got to get the money for any expenses from the House of Burgesses."

"I hear two or three planters up on the Northern Neck, Lawrence Washington for one, are enlisting and outfitting men at their own expense," added another. "Reckon they hope to be captains."

"Caribbean! That means the West Indies and the Spanish Main!" exclaimed yet another. "I've always wanted to see them."

"What I like," said Rob, "is the promise I heard that Americans would have share and share alike in any plunder taken from the enemy. Plunder is Spanish gold, pieces of eight, jewels, the riches of Peru! Remember what Drake and Morgan and those others used to get when they captured Spanish cities and treasure ships!"

"There's a good sized *if* in that," pointed out Tom thoughtfully. "*If* we can get them."

"Look here. Englishmen can beat Spaniards any day," Rob declared confidently. "Why, only last year Admiral Edward Vernon took Porto Bello with just a handful of ships."

"What's the war about anyway" asked a younger scholar timidly. "I don't understand."

"You should read the news from London in printer Parks' *Virginia Gazette*," one told him loftily. "All England is aroused against Spain again because the Spaniards haven't been keeping a treaty that allowed British ships to trade in certain ports in Spanish

America. They've been taking our ships on the high seas, claiming they were smugglers. That's the British side of it, at least."

"Ha!" snorted Tom. "I wouldnt' put it beyond some Englishmen to do a bit of smuggling if there was a profit in it. That goes for a lot of our people, too. Look at the land grabbing that goes on."

"But if the Spanish have been taking our ships for these past years, what brought it all to a head—started the war?" asked Greg.

"A sea captain named Jenkins appeared before Parliament with one of his ears preserved in a jar of spirits. He said it had been torn off seven years before by the captain of a Spanish coast guard ship who had boarded his vessel. The captain told him to take the ear to his king and tell him the Spanish would serve him in the same way if they ever got a chance. That set off a row. There was a big faction in Parliament that wanted another war with Spain and here was an excuse it could use to rouse the country and get Parliament to vote the money for the war."

Rob chuckled as a thought struck him. "Jenkins and his cut-off ear. You might call this the 'War of Jenkins' ear!' "

The others began to laugh. "Who ever heard such a name for a war?" "You could put it on a flag" "Make a ballad about it!"

"Well, it's no use our dreaming of fortunes to be made," sighed Greg, who had been seeing visions of piles of pieces of eight.

Further talk was interrupted by the sound of a dog's excited yapping and a woman's scream. Turning, they saw a frightened horse rear and jump to one side, sending the driver of a chaise tumbling out of his seat to the street. Reins flapping, the terrified beast bounded on a zigzag course that threatened to overturn the chaise at every leap. The dog pursued with happy barks.

Greg flung off his gown as he ran into the street, seized a trailing rein as it went by him and with a leap vaulted on to the horse's back. As he pulled hard on the rein he yelled to the others to drive off the dog, then managed to turn the horse to the sidewalk where, blocked by the door of a tavern, it halted, shivering with fright. Greg slid to the ground, seized the other rein and began gentling the horse with soft words and strokes.

The elderly driver arrived in a limping run. "You all right, Miz Mary?" he quavered.

"Law! I thought I was done for!" cried the plump lady in the chaise, fanning herself with a handkerchief. "That horse isn't safe! Frightened by a little dog! If it hadn't been for the young man I don't know what would have happened."

It had all taken place so quickly that Greg was surprised to find himself surrounded by his friends.

"Well done," Rob approved.

"Had no idea you were such a horseman," said John Mason admiringly.

Suddenly Greg felt weak in the knees—he hadn't either.

A man panted up to the chaise. "Mary!" he gasped. "Thank heaven you're safe. I was too far away to help."

"Oh, Jason, 'twas frightful," sobbed the lady. "Do thank that brave young man."

The man turned, bowed to Greg, then grasped him by the shoulders. The round face was flushed, the blue eyes serious. "I am deeply in your debt, young sir," he began. "You have saved my dear wife from harm." He glanced at the circle around them. "You are, I take it, of the college. May I ask your name?"

"I am Gregory Shelby, sir. My family lives northwest of here, near the Pamunkey."

"Shelby. Shelby," murmured the man. "Ah, yes. I knew of your father." He paused. "I am Jason Pollock, merchant. My house is on Francis Street. I can not thank you enough for what you have just done."

His tone was so earnest that Greg was embarrassed. "It's just natural to help when somebody is in trouble. Anyone could have stopped the horse."

"But no one else tried," murmured Mr. Pollock, as he introduced his wife. Greg bowed and hurried after his friends.

At the door of the college building he was stopped by the usher. "Your father is here, Shelby, waiting to see you. You may talk with him in the parlor."

Greg's breath caught in his throat. Was it his mother? What could have brought his father all the way to Williamsburg? He hurriedly entered the handsome square room.

John Shelby stood by a front window, his hands clasped behind his back. Greg paused. Though he and his father sometimes disagreed, he was old enough now, at sixteen, to realize that some of his father's impatience came from hard work on the plantation and worry about money. The place was too small. Unlike the large estates, Pine Grove's crop of tobacco was barely enough to keep its owner's credit in good standing with the tobacco factor when the annual settlement was made for the colony's chief export. Greg was almost sure that the cost of sending him to college was an additional strain on that credit. Only because both parents were determined that he should have a better life and rise in some profession was he here now. He looked at his father's best brown broadcloth coat and the white stock that he knew was darned where it did not show and felt a great sorrow.

"Father!" he said, and started across the room. "What has happened?"

He was shocked by the face his father turned to him. The brown eyes were sunk beneath their heavy brows and two lines of worry had deepened at the sides of his mouth. He caught Greg's arms in strong hands and looked at him eagerly but anxiously. "It's good to see you, Greg, though I have bad news. Not about your mother. She is well and sends her dear love. But I must tell you, and quickly. There will be no money for you to continue your studies here. We regret it, but it cannot be helped."

Greg felt as if someone had hit him in the stomach. "Leave college, for good?" he gasped.

"Yes, my boy, now, since the term has ended. There seems nothing else to do." John Shelby dropped his hands and turned back to the view of the lawn and the wide straight line of Duke of Gloucester street beyond. "Further, I must tell you that it is all my fault." He paused, and his quiet voice had a note of weariness when he resumed. "You remember the family named Higgins, the man who occasionally worked for me when I could pay him? They lived on the road to Fredericksburg."

Greg remembered. Mrs. Higgins, a worn and anxious woman, had once taken care of his mother when she was ill. He had never liked Lem Higgins.

"He came to me in great trouble last year; his only hogshead of tobacco was wormy; there was no food and another baby was coming. What could I do? I went on a note to Captain Bartlett for twenty-five pounds. Last week it fell due. I rode to the Higgins farm and found the place empty. A neighbor said that a month ago they had taken everything they owned in the wagon and headed west. Higgins had said he was going to find free land; that's all that is known."

"He never meant to pay," muttered Greg.

"Probably. I should have thought of that instead of his wife and five children. I rode immediately to see Captain Bartlett but found that he was here in Williamsburg, where he set up a shop a year or two ago. So I came to see him and explain the situation and that of course I meant to pay off the note in time."

He paused and took a deep breath. "This morning I talked with him. He . . . he laughed at me. He said he had thought I was a fool to sign the note. He will not wait for his money. If I cannot pay him now he will have to take a field. In fact, he'd sent his overseer to walk over our place as soon as he had heard that Higgins had disappeared. Only one field is worth twenty-five pounds, he said, and that is the south slope."

"But that's our best," cried Greg.

"Yes. He has already filed his claim at the courthouse and now his slaves will work the tobacco Will and I recently spent so much time and labor transplanting from the seed beds. Bartlett said that if I could pay him in ten years I could have the field back. But you know tobacco; by then the field will be worn out."

Greg did indeed know tobacco. It demanded hard work and infinite care in seeding, transplanting, cultivating, and curing. Also it wore out the land and was vulnerable to many kinds of disasters. He wished the weed had never been discovered. It had tied Virginia to a one-crop on-credit system which made money for the big landowners but little for the small ones.

"But it's not fair to take the field you've planted," protested Greg hotly. "There ought to be some way. . . ."

"But it's legal. I went to see lawyer Meadows to learn if aught could be done on my behalf. He says nothing can be. I have acknowledged I signed the note and neither Higgins nor I can pay it now it is due. Since I went surety I must satisfy the holder of the note in some way acceptable to him. The only thing he will accept is our finest field." He tried to smile. "So, my son, you understand. I can never tell you how much I regret this—this disaster. Your mother and I had so hoped that college would enable you to find a profession, but we shall be glad to have you home again. We need you. We will have to decide how much and what land to clear and plant and then get on with it."

He picked up his black tricorn hat from the sill and turned it around. "Oh, my boy, I am so sorry." The quiet voice broke.

Quickly Greg put his arm around his father's shoulders. "Don't feel so bad, father. We'll find a way out, clear some new fields, get good crops. Some way we'll work it out. You forget that Bartlett skinflint."

His father patted his hand absently. "We'll do our best together." A gong sounded from the buttery. "There. It is your dinner. I am going now to the President's house to tell Dr. Blair that you are leaving. After dinner pack your trunk. I will arrange to have it freighted to Pine Grove and will hire a horse for you to ride. There is no need to tell your friends more than that you are needed at home for a while. I will be back in an hour or so and we can take the road together." Another pat and he was gone.

In a daze Greg looked at the paneled walls, the big fireplace, the portrait, the sconces for candles. He had not realized how much he had enjoyed these months at college, how proud he had been to be a part of its life. And now it was over.

He squared his shoulders and hastened to the dining hall.

TWO

The King's Shilling

Across the field the pine trees shimmered in the heat. Greg straightened and wiped his forehead. The sun and the brazen sky were pressing down on the sandy earth with a weight one could almost feel. He had been in the fields since six and there were two hours more to go to noon and dinner. He had always known farming was hard work, after all it had filled most of his life, but after his months at Williamsburg it was harder than ever. Two rows away Will, more friend and servant than slave, was still hoeing steadily, and he could only admire his father's rhythmic strokes over at the edge of the pines.

Tomorrow they would top, which meant cutting the heads off the plants to keep them from blooming and stripping certain leaves so the rest of the leaves could grow strong and ripen. He told himself he would not mind farming so much if there was any end of it, or hope of real success. But it took a windfall or a stroke of great luck, or a steady income from a profession, to help a small planter.

The heat still held at dusk as the family gathered for supper. Greg scarcely listened to the quiet talk as he ate his share of the fish he had caught before breakfast, the corn bread and greens. Once his mother flashed him a smile as she pushed back the curly hair from her forehead. How pretty she is! he thought. She doesn't belong in a frame house spinning and weaving, helping with the cooking, caring for the garden day after day, year after year. And his father, with his learning and charm and honesty, should be a burgess, as he had once been, helping again to guide the colony. He smiled at them both. How much he owed them!

And in so many ways. Not only for the love and care and firmness with which he had been raised, but for the teaching which had made his entrance into college easy. His mother's father had been a tutor at Cambridge and had also taught his daughter well, so that, penniless at his death, she had easily found a place as governess. At the same manor house in Surrey John Shelby, once of Oxford, had been cataloguing the library. They had fallen in love, married, and with their savings set out for the new world where a man could be his own master and own his own land. Virginia had offered land and a climate that was mild, and they had bought four slaves, built a house and started a plantation. At first all had gone well, and John Shelby, liked and admired by his neighbors, had been elected to the House of Burgesses and served three terms. But the tobacco crop had failed for two years in succession, so he had been forced to devote his whole attention to farming. And this Captain Bartlett, who had arrived two years ago with many slaves and bought a thousand acres adjoining, had foreclosed on their best field!

Through all the years, no matter how many duties they had or how tired they might be, both his parents had tutored Greg steadily in Latin, history, mathematics, and the Bible. In the evenings they always read aloud for an hour from the store of books brought from England. So, when he had gone to college on carefully hoarded savings, he had been better prepared than many students and found he enjoyed learning for learning's sake. Law would have been the next step, but now. . . .

"Greg!" His mother's voice had a happy lilt. "You haven't been listening!"

Her smile was affectionate. He knew how much she had hoped for him, but when he had come back from college she had given him a quick hug and murmured, "My dear boy; we'll find some way," and never mentioned college again, for which he was grateful.

"Yes, ma'am," Greg smiled back and turned to his father.

"We have a commission, and a trip for you." His father's eyes were twinkling. "We need some household goods, and since the journey is tiring for me, we are sending you, with Will, to Williamsburg for us. Next month. We can spare you an extra day to see your friends. You would like that?"

They had plotted this to give him a change, Greg knew. What they did not remember was that his friends would be leaving late in July for the St. James's Day vacation and would not be back until St. Luke's Day soon after mid-October. He could not tell them that, or show he understood their ruse. "That will be splendid," he said quickly.

"Sweets for me, oh, please, Mother, put sweets on the list," begged Susan. "I haven't had any from a store in a long time."

"Sweets there will be for Susan," Greg promised the entreating little face across the table. Once there had been another sister and a small brother, but they had died of a malignant fever no herbs could cure. Susan was gay and engaging; no wonder they all spoiled her.

July passed into August. A drought lay over the hot land; there would be no surplus at Pine Grove this year. At last, one daybreak, Will brought horse and wagon to the front door. In the half-light his parents looked weary as he kissed them goodby.

"Take care of yourself," said his mother. "Just get what you can on the list; work down as far as the money holds out."

"Enjoy yourself." His father laid a hand on Greg's shoulder.

"Yes, sir, and, and thank you both." Greg wanted to say more, but the words would not come and he climbed to the seat by Will.

The afternoon of the second day they drew up before Connally's ordinary outside the town; the charges here were cheaper than in Williamsburg. Though there was no real reason to hurry, Greg went immediately to the store and soon had all the things on the short list—tea, sugar, molasses, a new kettle, a blade for a plow and one for an axe—set aside for Will to gather the next day. The lengths of cotton cloth, needles, thread, and buttons took longer, but at last all was bought.

His errands finished, Greg was at a loss for what to do; it was forlorn being in town with no friends. Resolutely he turned his

glance away from the college and began to stroll down the Duke of Gloucester Street. Somewhere he might run into someone he knew. In front of the printing office where Mr. Parks issued his weekly *Virginia Gazette,* and which was the news center for the town, his back was slapped suddenly.

"Greg Shelby! It's good to see you!" It was Jack Caruthers, a day student at the college. Greg shook hands with more enthusiasm than he had ever felt for Jack before.

"Here," Jack drew him to a group of men in front of the small-paned window. "Let's listen. Only way to find out anything without paying for a paper. They're saying our troops will be leaving soon."

"For where" Greg asked. He'd forgotten all about the war with Spain. "What's been happening?"

"Nothing much, so far. Governor Gooch has raised four hundred men from Virginia. They're camped outside the town now. Sometimes they come in to drill on the square. Former Governor Spotswood was to command all the American troops, but he died, perhaps you heard, on his way north to inspect troops in the other colonies. Now Governor Gooch is going to be in command."

They listened to the talk for a few minutes but it was on crops and politics and they moved away. "Wish I could go to the war," Jack observed wistfully. "Excitement. New lands. Adventure. Loot. Someone said the French freebooter who took Cartagena in 1696 got a million pounds ransom for the place."

"Are the troops going to Cartagena?" asked Greg, who remembered now the reports of the British promise that Americans would share equally in the plunder.

"No one knows, yet. But it's a good target, after Admiral Vernon's taking Porto Bello last year. A big English fleet and a lot of soldiers are going to Jamaica, so our men will, too."

Though he could ill spare the cost from his pocket money, Greg agreed to have supper at the Raleigh Tavern with Jack. He was a gossip and between him and the talk at the Tavern Greg was sure he would learn news of the colony to take home.

The taproom was hot, crowded, smoke-filled. They found a corner where they could take their time over their meal. At first Jack rattled on about their friends, and when he turned to girls, most of

whom Greg did not know, Greg could watch the five men at the
next table as they puffed at their long clay pipes and laughed over
their tankards of ale. His father should be in such a group. But how
could that ever happen again? There was no plunder in Williamsburg, and Greg knew that for him the life of a lawyer who made
good fees was as far away as the moon. But he nodded and smiled
to Jack at any pause and listened to the talk of the men: the price
of tobacco would go up (or down), a new horse named Pimlico
had won a race, the Council had appointed three of the captains
for the troops, the Governor would soon put an end to the Assembly, rain was needed. At last Jack said he must get home and Greg
walked with him to the door.

On his way back to Connally's ordinary, under a full moon that
turned the road to pale gold between the tree shadows, Greg's mind
was still burdened with the problem of his family and the future.
He was the only son. It was up to him to do something. The sad
gobbling calls of whippoorwills from the woods seemed to mock
him.

In the morning Greg strolled back to town. He had still to hear
news of the war, and there were Susan's sweets to purchase.

On the green at the powder magazine a group had gathered
around a sergeant who was exhorting a shambling country boy to
enlist with the Virginia troops.

"Come, take the King's shilling, my lad," the sergeant was coax-
ing. "You'll get bounty money and soldier's pay besides and a share
of the great plunder. And you only sign on for two years!"

"But there might be fighting," objected the boy uneasily.

"It's Spaniards you'll be fighting. Not one of them can stand up
to an English musket with an Englishman behind it. They never
have. Whatever city we go against will fall like a plum into our
hands."

The boy shook his head and moved away. The sergeant hailed
Greg. "Now, young sir, you're a likely one, well-set-up, strong,
handsome, you'd make a fine looking soldier. Line up for Virginia
and England and make your fortune while you're doing it."

Startled, Greg stared at the man. He had never considered enlisting. No, he was needed at home. And yet. . . . All his nagging

worries about the family's financial plight suddenly came into focus. This might, just possibly might, be the way out. If the spoils were big enough it could be the answer. He remembered the Frenchman's million-pound ransom for Cartagena. Certainly a part of such a sum would trickle down to the ranks. "I'll have to think about it," he told the man seriously.

"Better think fast then. I need only four to fill the ranks. Four daisy pickers went home sick yesterday—only reason there's vacancies."

"I'll have to think," repeated Greg, and turned away.

"Well, if it isn't young Mr. Shelby who stopped the runaway horse," exclaimed a pleasant voice, and Greg recognized the merchant.

"And you are Mr. Pollock," said Greg politely.

"Right, my boy. But I wouldn't have expected to see you in town until your return to college in October."

"I—I'm here on an errand, sir." Greg hesitated. "I won't be back at college in the autumn."

The round face looked surprised. "After your brave deed I spoke to your teachers and found you were an excellent student. You should go on."

"I know, sir, but—but my father needs me at home."

"Oh," and the other was silent for a moment. "Come over here where we can talk." Greg followed him away from the center of the green. "Now," went on Mr. Pollock. "I'd like to know the trouble, if you feel you can tell me."

Greg knew he liked this man and could speak frankly. "There have been, well, reverses at home. My father doesn't have the money to send me back to college."

"Ummm." The merchant pulled at his plump chin. "When the sergeant was speaking to you I sensed you were hesitating. Have you really thought of enlisting for the West Indies expedition?"

"I hadn't. But I've been worrying about the family and the plantation and wondering what I could do to help get us out of—of our situation. All at once it came to me that this might be the way, with luck."

"Yes, with luck. But a long shot." The blue eyes were friendly but shrewd, and the voice became more grave. "I surely would not wish to advise you to any course that your family would not approve, or that would endanger you. The decision about enlisting is yours alone to make. Judge it carefully before you decide. But if you *do* join the expedition, I can offer you a commission for doing something for me in Jamaica. It is honorable, I assure you."

"What sort of commission, sir?"

"No need to tell you until you have decided. But it would be worth five pounds to me now and five more when you return and have done what is needed."

Greg tried to keep his face impassive. Five pounds now! His father could hire extra help for the harvest and have some money left over for spring planting. Five more pounds when the expedition was over! Meanwhile, a soldier's pay and the chance of much more . . . But to go off, leave home, give pain and worry to his mother and father . . . How could he do that?

"When do the troops sail?" he asked.

"They are due to leave sometime next month, September, I have heard. But, as the sergeant said, they must fill the ranks now. Recruits must learn the discipline and the drill. If he does not get his recruits in the next few hours he will by nightfall, with a free noggin or so of ale to aid him."

"I must ponder this," mumbled Greg.

"Do so, most carefully. Then, if you are interested in my offer, you will find me on Francis Street, there, the second house from the corner of Blair Street. Now, good luck, my boy, whichever course you choose." His smile as they separated was warm.

Greg headed for one of his favorite spots just outside the town, a pool of a small brook which he had sought in the past when he needed to be alone and think. If ever he needed to think it was now. He flung himself down in the cooling shade of the trees and watched the flowing water while he turned over in his mind the pro's and con's of the problem. He did not want to hurt his mother and father, and they needed his help on the farm. But he could see no future in his present course, for himself or for them. On the other hand, he would be taking a wild chance, might get himself killed, with no benefit to anyone. There was the glittering possibility of gain, but the hard part of his mind told him this was only a possibility; he might come home penniless.

His thoughts went round and round, considering alternatives. None seemed any good: it must be either the expedition or the farm. If he joined the army he would, of course, tell his parents at once. That would bring his father to Williamsburg to try to change his decision. Yet, he was sure, once you were in the army there was no way out without more influence than his father had now.

Greg sat up and rested his chin on his knees as he watched the shining flecks of sunlight on the water. There was the merchant's offer. What would he have to do? At least it would be honest, and would mean cash money he could send to his father now by Will, along with a letter explaining everything. That would be a tangible gain, anyway. Suddenly, his mind made up, he sprang to his feet and started back to the powder magazine.

He found the sergeant swearing in a recruit, a seedy looking fellow of about thirty, and sending him off to the camp.

It was soon done. Greg signed his name to a muster roll, raised his hand to a gabbled oath of allegiance, pocketed the King's shilling, and was reluctantly granted leave to report the next morning so he could set his affairs in order. It was growing late. Now for Mr. Pollock.

He walked quickly down Francis Street toward the corner of Blair Street. He had made up his mind; he must never look back. But now his whole life would be different. He would be seeing strange places, strange people, and the warm familiar life of home and college would be around him no more. At that last thought something caught at his throat. He stopped a minute. Two ladies, parasols aslant, deep in quick talk, went by, then a laundry-woman pulling a washbasket on a little homemade cart. Two small boys chased each other across the street and down an alley. Doggedly, Greg went forward. He had committed himself to one thing, soon he would be committed to another. A countryman with a red, weathered face was leading his son by the hand and pointing over to Duke of Gloucester Street. At the next house a man was leaning against the fence corner whittling at a piece of wood which looked as if it would become a whistle. It was unusual to see anyone so idle on the street and Greg looked from the whistle to the man. He was thin and not very tall, with reddish hair above a freckled face. The eyes that glanced at Greg indifferently were a pale blue. As Greg turned into the marl walk between the picket fence he glanced back. The man had stopped whittling and was watching him.

Mr. Pollock's house was white and neat, with dormer windows set in gables above the first floor, a brick kitchen at the rear and a grape arbor in the garden beyond. At Greg's knock a servant girl opened the door. On one side of the entrance hall was the merchant's stock room and office, for this house, like a number in Williamsburg, served both as dwelling and place of business. Mr. Pollock beamed as he rose from behind a handsome desk and shook hands.

"Ah, my boy. You have made your choice. I am glad, for my own sake, and I wish you good fortune. Here, sit in this chair. You naturally wish to know what sort of commission I have in mind."

"Yes, sir," Greg agreed a little uneasily. He was beginning to wonder if he had been right, but told himself firmly he must not look back, now or in the future.

The merchant returned to his arm chair and placed his finger tips gently together as he nodded approvingly. "Quite right. The commission, for which I will pay you five pounds now and another five when you return, is to take a letter to my business associate in Jamaica. His name is Mr. James Woodford, and he has an office in Kingston. I will explain why I need a special messenger for this letter and why I have chosen you." He paused long enough to light a candle, for the sun had set.

"In the first place, Williamsburg, important to Virginia as it is, is a small town as far as foreign trade goes compared to New York, Boston, or Philadelphia, and has few opportunities for a trader. Since the wealthy planters here send their import trade to their factors in England, where they can buy against their stocks of tobacco those same factors sell for them, the business for a man not allied with an English house is small. But sales are possible if goods are on hand to show.

"I trade with the West Indies and England, sending out staples and importing whatever is moderately profitable, if the cargoes arrive. Sometimes special goods are ordered. I can either send for what is needed or accept what Mr. Woodford can find to ship, and if there is no market here I can forward to other cities. I make a modest living. But two years ago there settled here another merchant who also deals in whatever comes his way. He is, I must admit, more venturesome than I am, he has more capital, and is in closer touch with what is called the 'sloop trade,' the coastal vessels of moderate size which carry cargoes between the Caribbean islands and the mainland. I am also beginning to believe that he has friends among the so-called privateers whose network of spies keeps them informed of sailings. This enables these pirates to capture the light and practically unarmed merchant ships, with their cargoes, both of which can all be sold at great profit. I know that small ships slip up the river, anchor for a night or two, unload cargoes by boats, and vanish. It is only my own supposition that allies such ships to smugglers, but that explains in part the need for secrecy.

"As to why I have chosen you . . . I must, in all fairness, tell you that two of my letters to Mr. Woodford, entrusted to the mates of ships, never arrived—letters that certainly were bought or stolen. Next, my own clerk vanished from his ship, perhaps lured away, but the result has been that three cargoes I needed have not come. So it occurred to me that by choosing an inconspicuous lad, one of four hundred soldiers bound for Jamaica, the chances of your being connected with me are small and you will succeed in delivering my letter."

Greg felt a moment of pity for this round, courageous little man struggling against some powers he could not overcome. "That seems very sensible, sir," he approved warmly. "I'll see the letter arrives safely."

"Good. It is important to me, for my stock is low and there are debts." The arched fingers tightened. "My wife is fond of Williamsburg and I would not care to be forced to leave. One, two cargoes will set things to rights."

"Who is this other merchant here" asked Greg.

Mr. Pollock hesitated. "Perhaps I should not have said so much. He has set himself up well and acts the gentleman with money, but he is no real gentleman. He has a plantation to the north and a shop here where he is seldom seen. He calls the shop "Travis and Son," but he calls himself Captain Bartlett."

"But that's the man who took the best field from my father!" Greg cried.

"Really?" Mr. Pollock looked over the edge of his glasses. "I am not surprised. He is ruthless, and the men who work for him must be also."

"I'll do anything to help you against Captain Bartlett."

"Good. So we are allies in more ways than one. On the other hand, Mr. Woodford you will find an honorable gentleman; he is also experienced and kindly. You may trust him in anything. This I know, though we have never met in person.

"When my letter is ready I will send you word by my boy and you will come here for it. It will be wrapped in oilskin to protect it and will be so small it will not discommode you. I will have it sewed in a money belt for you to wear always. Finally, I will then give you the password. Yes," he smiled mischievously, "that sounds mysterious, and I confess I enjoy it, but it has seemed to me necessary."

He unlocked a drawer of his desk. "And now," he coughed delicately, "I would like to make the down payment, if that is agreeable to you."

"Yes, sir," replied Greg, appreciating the tact of the man.

Mr. Pollock took an iron box from the drawer, unlocked it, and began counting coins of different kinds, most of them pieces of eight or shillings. Greg watched, keeping tally in his head, and nodded agreement when the pile was completed. The merchant smiled approvingly, locked and replaced the box and produced a small cotton sack from another drawer.

"You'll need this to carry the coins. It has grown almost dark and if you leave by the garden gate no one will notice you. We must take care to keep our arrangement secret." He rose and shook hands fervently. "Good luck, my boy."

Mr. Pollock opened the back door to show the garden path and Greg realized that for a moment they were both silhouetted against the light. The door closed, his feet found the brick walk. As he opened the garden gate he peered at the high bayberry bushes on either side. Anyone could be in those deep shadows, watching, waiting. The back of his neck prickled as he fancied he heard a slight rustle. Telling himself firmly that it was only the wind and not to start imagining dangers, he hurried into the street.

Once there Greg paused. He should return promptly to camp, but it would be months, perhaps years, before he saw Williamsburg again. He had not realized how much he cared for it until now it was going out of his life. The heart of town was Duke of Gloucester Street; it would do no harm to walk a few blocks there, to look up once more at the College and back at the Capitol as his own private farewell to town and college.

The deep dusk and the lights from the windows, soft and glowing, lent an air of mystery and a touch of sadness to match his somber mood as he walked along Duke of Gloucester Street. He strolled slowly, glancing at the various people and houses he passed. Ahead, the Red Lion Tavern was more brightly lit. He skirted a group of men discussing ships and cargoes and glanced again at the tavern, where arguments of all kinds went on day and night. From the suddenly opened door light fell on two men standing before it. One was big, with wide shoulders, head thrust forward on a short neck and a shining coat of green. Greg recognized Captain Bartlett. The man he was talking to was weedy and his hair was reddish. Greg quickened his pace. He could not bear to look at Bartlett, or, by any remote chance, be recognized by him.

The next morning Will was at first unbelieving when Greg told him what he had done. "I don't like it, Mr. Greg. An' they won't like it either. You goin' off to heathen parts this way. An' it's me that's got to tell them." He kept shaking his head and muttering protests as they loaded the wagon.

Greg gave him the sack of coins, saving out three shillings in case his army pay did not come soon, and, last, the letter he had spent much of the night writing. He watched the wagon out of sight. Then he set out for the camp of the Virginia companies.

THREE

To the Spanish Main

AFTER a few days Greg began to grow accustomed to his new life. The camp, at the edge of a large grove of oaks, consisted of eight rows of neatly pitched tents with their entrances facing on the four company streets. At the ends of the rows were tents for the officers and sergeants.

Greg had been assigned to a company commanded by Captain Charles Walker, a regular army officer from England who had been appointed by the Governor. The other three captains were Virginians; Lawrence Washington, who had been educated in England and had an estate on the Potomac; Richard Bushrod, a well-to-do planter from Westmoreland County, who had raised his own company, and James Mercer, a lawyer. Each company of about 100 men and officers had two lieutenants, one ensign, four corporals and two drummers, as well as the four sergeants, one of them a British regular assigned from the garrison of New York.

The enlisted men were a varied lot. Many were volunteers who had joined out of patriotism, or love of adventure, or hope of loot. But there had not been enough of these to fill the ranks. Others—too many of them thought Greg—were ex-convicts who had been shipped out from England to the colonies to get rid of them, or men of no occupation who had been impressed, under orders, by sheriffs or justices of the peace. Greg's particular mentor was one of his six tentmates, a stocky, bright-eyed, older man named Jed Bunnell who had served in both the British army and navy.

The first morning a pile of clothes and strange objects had been heaped in Greg's arms and he'd been told briskly to take them to his tent, get dressed, and learn the equipment of a British soldier. He had carried it all back awkwardly and dumped the collection on his pallet. Jed found him looking at it in dismay.

"I can see it's all new to a young gentleman like you," he had said in a business-like voice. "Here's your uniform."

Greg had pulled out the red coat with green cuffs and lapels, red waistcoat, one of the two pairs of red breeches, cocked hat (which he rather fancied), long white gaiters and low shoes, and had awkwardly put them on.

When he had finished Jed nodded. "Fells strange, don't it? But you won't know the difference soon. Now. Here's your knapsack, cowhide it is, canteen, and canvas haversack to carry what's left over. This here's a hanger, you hang it on your waist belt to hold that bayonet. Cartridge box goes on the bandolier over your shoulder. Seems a lot to carry, but it's not as much as some regulars. Some got to carry entrenching tools with 'em all the time. Get everything lined up straight now. Me, I know too much about it. I'll see you get started right. There's not much time before we leave and sergeants, let me tell you, are short-tempered men. You'll get your musket at drill this afternoon."

His new friend had then given Greg some quick instructions in the formal drill he would have to learn and the orders he would hear. Greg was grateful later when one of the sergeants began bellowing hoarse and incomprehensible orders which otherwise would have bewildered him completely. But he thought he had the hang of it by the end of the first day and further coaching from Jed helped.

The weather suddenly turned cool and it began raining. The drill field became a sea of mud, but the drilling went on when the showers stopped. There was much grumbling among the men at having to dry and clean their equipment after each mud bath, and

Greg found himself muttering with them, though Jed never complained. Greg noticed that the officers spent as much time as they could in Williamsburg, leaving the camp in charge of the sergeants, and he envied them and yearned for the dry comfortable rooms of the college.

The expected visit from his father came a week after Greg's enlistment. The interview was painful, for John Shelby blamed himself for Greg's decision. He had thought of going to a lawyer, his father said, to see if there was any way of getting Greg released, but had decided nothing could be done. And now he believed he understood the several reasons why Greg had joined up.

"There is one thing, however, that worries me and could make me change my mind. Why is this merchant, Mr. Pollock, paying you five pounds?"

"That I cannot tell you, father, but it involves nothing dishonest. He is paying me for a service that is entirely proper."

"In that case I will use the money to hire a man for the tobacco picking and will keep him on to clear the west tract for planting next year."

"How—how does mother feel about this?" asked Greg, touched by his father's trust.

"She is worried, of course, but tries not to show it. She sends her dear love and pleads that you take care of yourself in foreign lands and will pray for your safe return. We know letters are uncertain, but we will hope to hear from you when you can write. And remember you have our love and thoughts and blessings with you always."

Greg was near to tears as he and his father shook hands and embraced. "I—I think, father, this will turn out all right. I'm going to bring back enough money, somehow, to solve our problems. Give mother my love and tell her I'll try to take care."

"We will be praying for your safe return. Goodby, my son."

For some days Greg had no chance to leave camp. There were drills and guard duty and inspections. He became quite proficient at drill, which pleased him. He got on well with most of the volunteers, but there was a surly, older group he did not like, men with hard wizened faces who muttered curses at every order or reprimand. "Old lags," Jed called them, "ex-convicts, some of 'em for political reasons, others as stole a loaf of bread or poached on a lord's deer park. An' some for worse than that. Shipped to the colonies an' now the colonies are getting rid of 'em in their own way. It's the system. They're not good soldiers, an' never will be, nor good companions in camp *or* in a fight."

Word came that ships were gathering at Norfolk to take the troops to Jamaica, so he was not surprised when a small, neatly dressed boy sidled up to him as he was chopping wood and said in a casual voice, but with the happy gleam of a conspirator, that it was hoped he could come into town that evening. Greg grinned and whispered he'd get there.

It was quite dark before he approached the house on Francis Street. The merchant welcomed him and immediately produced the money belt containing the letter.

"Keep this tied around you," he warned again. "Never let it leave your person for any reason. See, it both ties and buckles. When you reach Kingston go at your first opportunity to Mr. Woodford's office on Prince Street and deliver it to him yourself. But before you hand it to him say 'The wind seems to be from the north.' He will reply, 'But soon it will be from the east and then from the south! Repeat them both, please."

Greg complied; they would be easy to remember.

There was bustle and confusion and some grumbling at the work involved when the four companies struck camp. Greg and Jed were struggling with the unwieldy canvas of their tent when a voice beside them said "Jed Bunnell! Would have known you anywhere!"

Jed's head jerked up. A thin man in what looked like a new uniform was watching them from pale eyes under the tricorn hat. "Vizer Bates," grunted Jed. "Could say the same for you. What you doing here?"

Greg glanced at the stranger and with mild surprise recognized the man who had been leaning against the fence whittling near Mr. Pollock's house the afternoon after Greg had enlisted.

"Sergeant caught me at the tavern last night," replied the newcomer. "Needed a replacement, he said, and me without a penny to wet my whistle. Found out I knew the drill from times past, and here I am, in Captain Bushrod's company. Who's your friend?"

Jed pulled the canvas further from the man. "Name of Greg Shelby. Why ain't you striking camp?"

"Don't have a tent to strike," said the other smugly. "I'm just looking around. I'll see you later." He slouched away.

"Not if I can help it," muttered Jed.

"Who's that?" Greg asked.

"He was around last spring, looking for work like I was, but he weren't so particular about what kind, from what I heard. Did some jobs for some planter. I'm kind of surprised he joined up. Don't like him." The short man's face was red and he was punching the canvas flat with hard blows of his fist.

"We won't likely see him again for a while," said Greg, "since he's in a different company." He was wondering at the circumstance of the man joining up at the last moment. Yet it could be merely coincidence.

"Any time's too soon. Git that canvas down and stomp on it, only way to git it into shape."

When the dismantling of the camp was finished the four companies marched to the green in Williamsburg where, to the beating of drums, they paraded before Governor Gooch. As the column of troops passed down Duke of Gloucester Street and turned by the Capitol, Greg felt a sudden let-down. What was he doing with these tramping men? It was all strange and alien and he felt very foolish. He wondered if he would ever see Williamsburg again.

The Virginia troops marched to four waiting transports and sailed for Norfolk. After several days at anchor there the men in Greg's transport, which had Governor Gooch aboard, and those in the other vessels, were growing heartily tired of their cramped quarters. They had been joined by H.M.S. *Wolfe*, a sloop of war that carried twelve guns, for defense against Spaniards or privateers. Commanded by Captain Dandridge, a Virginian, it was to be their escort.

All were waiting for the remainder of the flotilla and also for

overdue supplies bought on Governor Gooch's personal credit. The Assembly had voted money to pay for transportation of the soldiers, but there seemed to be something wrong with the British commissary system, for it had failed to supply promised rations for the troops. It was the colonials' first experience of the trouble they were to have merely getting enough to eat.

By the time the local supplies were loaded, five other vessels, with Maryland and Pennsylvania militia aboard, had arrived, and on October 2nd the fleet of 10 sail got under way. Greg watched in amazement as some sailors strained at the capstan to raise the anchor, others ran up the ratlines to shake out the sails, and still others hauled at the hanging shrouds as they squared away before the wind. The very thought of climbing to the swaying heights above and then standing on ropes to make or shorten sail turned him dizzy. With Governor Gooch's transport leading, the ships passed between the capes of the Chesapeake and began gentle up and down and rolling motions as they met the swells of the Atlantic.

Greg was standing at the rail, glad to be free of the dark odorous hold and to feel the sea wind on his face. He had never been on any water but a river, or in any boat but a canoe or barge. "A lot of water," he remarked uneasily to Jed, eyeing the boundless waste before them.

"You'll see a lot more," was Jed's sour reply. "An' none of it any good except to sail on or to go under when a storm sinks you."

"Storms?"

"On the Western Ocean can be anything," Jed went on with glum pleasure in his forebodings. "Hurricane season's on. Sink ships without trace, they do. There's water spouts, stay away from them, an' ordinary storms with waves forty feet high; they're not healthful either." He went on to tell of a blow that had lasted a week somewhere out in mid-ocean, and by the time he had finished Greg's hair was on end.

"I don't feel it yet," remarked an upcountry militiaman who had been listening, "but I've heard tell a man can get awful sea sick."

"Some do, some don't," Jed agreed judiciously. "Depends on the man. Some has sea legs from the beginning and some don't never get them. But in a real storm anybody's like to feel queasy."

As they sailed south the water grew bluer and the air softer. They were entering a great current, Jed said, that came up from the tropics and, some believed, went all the way across the Atlantic to Europe, though no one explained how. It was hard to get used to only two meals a day and to sleeping at night as tightly packed as pickets in a fence. But discipline was easy and there was a growing feeling of adventure among many of the men.

One morning as the first meal of the day was ending and the corporals were seeing to it that the fires on the cooking hearths were put out and that the water candles—vertical tubes filled with water to hold a floating piece of wax candle—were pinched and stowed, Sergeant Simmons appeared. "Attention!" he called. "Who here can read—and read well?"

There was a stunned silence.

"It's not usual," the Sergeant conceded, "it's a special duty." His glance, shifting from face to face, rested on Greg. "You. Shelby. You joined at Williamsburg. Heard you'd been to the college. You may do. Report to Ensign Young, and look as neat as you can."

"You can't ask him what for," muttered Jed as Greg opened his mouth. "Wash up and go along."

Ensign Young, a blond, anxious looking, youthful man, was in a small cabin. "It is the Governor himself who wishes you," he began in a voice so low and soft against the creaking of the yards above and the sloshing of waves against the hull that Greg could hardly hear him. "He wants someone to read to him. He—he does not care for the voices he has tried. He is—er—seasick, you understand. He never gets over it, no matter how many times he is aboard ship or for how long. He does not feel well enough to read to himself. You must do your best—and be discreet about this, Shelby."

The cabin, in the stern, was pleasantly cooled by the breeze that swept through the open windows. The Governor, in a loose white shirt and trousers, his hair clubbed, sat in an armchair. His eyes were closed and his face was pale.

"This is Private Gregory Shelby, sir," announced the Lieutenant a little stiffly. "He has been a student at the college."

The Governor opened his large brown eyes, surveyed Greg and tried to smile, then closed his eyes again. "Shelby, Shelby," he murmured. "Any relation of John Shelby who was once a burgess?"

"He is my father, sir," Greg said proudly.

"Ah, yes. I remember him and his charming wife. He is a learned man. His son should be able to read well." He paused, then went on in a tone of pained amusement. "Unlike Councilor William Byrd of Westover, who daily reads Greek and Hebrew, or Latin and French, you need only to read English, but it must be so clearly done as to engage my thoughts."

He lifted a long hand and pointed to a book on a table by a window and a straight chair beside it. "This cursed seasickness will be the death of me—at times I hope it will. No matter. When I am sufficiently distracted from it, so I do not watch the horizon go up and down, I sometimes feel a little better. That book is by Sir Hans Sloane, who came to the West Indies fifty years ago. It is still the best book on Jamaica. My brother sent it to me this spring, with some others, for my entertainment. Perhaps he thought the illustrations would amuse me. Turn past the preface—it is about the ill persons he has cured—and the introduction, and start with his own tale."

Greg sat down and ran his fingers over the smooth leather binding of the large folio volume. He opened to the crowded title page, turned then to the proper page, and began to read: "On Monday, the 12 day of September 1687 I went on Board the Assistance Frigate one of the King's ships of 44 guns and 200 men . . ." On the second page the then Dr. Sloane took up seasickness. At the word the Governor opened his eyes. "Eh? What's that? He says that only one in 50 escapes? Good. Read again about there being no remedies. Only keeping quiet, you read, in a place of least motion without noisome smell or sight? Then it is hopeless." He closed his eyes but listened intently to the various cures advocated, which did no good, and murmured "Poor man!" when the author confessed that he had been seasick steadily for a month going to Jamaica and the six weeks returning.

At the end of an hour, when Greg was growing hoarse, the Governor dismissed him with a compliment on his reading and said he would send for him that afternoon. So twice a day Greg read to Governor Gooch, going through Dr. Sloane's experiences and the brief history of the islands and stopping when they came to the pages that began listing the flora and fauna complete with Latin names. They turned next to *Essay on Man* by Alexander Pope, which Greg found heavy going, but which the Governor enjoyed.

Of all the company Jed was the most at home on the ship and the least affected by the smothering heat and foul smells below deck. He attributed his good fortune to his years as a sailor, but allowed it took more time to get used to life on a ship than he cared to remember. It was he who one day pointed to a low dim blur on the horizon and announced it was the eastern tip of the island of Cuba. When he said it was big, 700 miles long, east to west, some of the men didn't believe him.

"All the same, it's so," Jed told them flatly. " 'Tis Cuba we're passing an' we're lucky we're so many sail, for no blasted Spanish guardacosta will bother us. An' that's not all, ye ignorant landlubbers. It means that if the wind holds, an' it generally does in these parts, we'll be at Port Royal, Jamaica, in three days at most." After that he lapsed into a sulky silence.

Greg and Jed were at the rail on the morning of the second day when the lookout on the foremast shouted "Land ho!" and pointed southwest. Jed shaded his eyes and gave a grunt of satisfaction. All the soldiers scrambled from below decks to see soon a faintly discernible blue object on the edge of the horizon.

"The Blue Mountains," said Jed, "an' rightly named. Prettiest things you'll see in Jamaica, if you stay at a distance from them."

As the hours passed the mountains rose steadily out of the sea until by late afternoon, as they drew near shore, Greg could see they were thickly forested and that white threads of waterfalls plunged down their sides. Scallops of white beaches stood out against the glittering water and little boats with colored sails scudded along near shore. Clearings above some of the beaches showed white houses and above all loomed the towering blue peaks.

Greg pointed inquiringly to the sailboats. "Coast trade," muttered Jed. "At least most of them. Planters have to go by boat; can't go over *or* around the mountains, not with any ease. Could be other boats, too. There's a lot of the old pirate strain still here. Cut your throat for a groat." He raised his eyes to the mountains again and was silent as their transport stood out from shore to round a long, low peninsula at the eastern end of the island.

He did not speak again until a sports enthusiast asked about the hunting. Jed told him grumpily that there was nothing to shoot but wild pigs and ducks, adding that there were sharks in the waters and alligators in the rivers and marshes. The depressed hunter shook his head: what sort of a place were they coming to, anyway?

That night the fleet lay with furled sails and the next morning, with a native pilot to guide them, the ships rounded a sand bank and entered a magnificent harbor.

"I never saw anything like it," gasped Greg.

"Not likely to, either," Jed told him. "I've heard there ain't many like it anywhere. Could hold all the King's navy, with lots of room to spare."

They passed a stone fort with the muzzles of cannon in its embrasures and were nearing a cluster of small houses beside a church. To their left the harbor stretched two miles or more, and ahead it extended a much greater distance to where the flat line of the peninsula turned to join the higher land and foothills. Across, on the opposite shore, stood a square town of white houses backed by rising hills with scattered buildings on the slopes. The high mountains were hidden by clouds, but around the bay everything was blue and green and bright.

"Not all it looks," said Jed. "Bugs that bite. Cockroaches, big ones. Moths. Snakes. Forests so thick with vines you can't walk through 'em. Swamps filled with what they call mangrove trees with roots that come right up out of the water and you can't get through them, neither. That town's Kingston."

"Where's Port Royal?" asked Greg, eager to keep the other talking.

Jed pointed to the fort and group of houses. "What you see there's all that's left of it. Notice how the pilot's been keeping out from land a bit? That's because of shoals where most of old Port Royal lies under water. There she was on that spit of land. Fool place to build a town—no wood, no water save what they caught when it rained, everything had to come in by boat. Except it was safe, see, for them days. Ships couldn't get in at that place through that narrow entrance with cannon shooting at them. When we took Jamaica from Spain, in the time of Cromwell that was, we made Port Royal our strongest place out here. It grew, merchants, ordinary folk, at first, and pirates who came to drink and carouse and spend the fortunes they'd taken from the Spaniards.

"Henry Morgan, what was a pirate 'til he sacked Panama an' then the King made him a knight, ruled the island an' the seas from Port Royal. He was a tough, hard man, but Port Royal prospered as long as he lived. Fifty years ago, 'tis said, there were two thousand houses here, taverns, merchants, rich, poor, the King's warehouse, docks, navy yard. In Jamaica they'll tell you the town was so wicked it was destroyed by the hand of God. Don't know about that, but it sure was destroyed. You've heard about it?"

"Go on," Greg urged, fascinated by the tale.

"Well, in 1692 (they won't let you forget the date) one mid-morning came a great earthquake. The main streets, forts, warehouses, most of the people went right down into the harbor, matter of seconds it was. Came another shock and more of the place slid into the water an' mud. Earthquakes shook the whole island."

"Then what happened?"

Jed spat over the rail. "Oh, they built it up, some, but ten years later came a big fire. Narrow streets—wood houses—no water—place went up in smoke. What little was left is about what you see now. End of Port Royal, 'cept as a place to careen ships. People moved to Kingston. That's where we're going now, 'cause we got to go into camp somewhere."

"How do you know?"

Jed looked at him pityingly. "Use your eyes. There's some sloops in the harbor but nary a man of war or transport. That means Admiral Vernon's ships that are based here must be out combing the seas for Spaniards or French. An' that means the big fleet from England, with troops, hasn't got here yet."

This was good news, in a way, for it would allow him extra time to find Mr. Woodford, thought Greg.

F O U R

Mr. Woodford of Kingston

THE sparkling brightness of the wavelets in the harbor, the glare of the sunlight, and the heavy dampness of the heat all contributed to a sense of strange, somewhat oppressive beauty as the troops stood on deck waiting for the ferries to take them across the bay. It was nearly November, yet it was as hot as a summer day in Virginia. A breeze, blowing down steadily from the hills back of the harbor, moderated the heat to some extent. Without that, Greg thought, it might be hard to move and live here.

At the wharves of Kingston the men went ashore and marched through the town and around a shallow bay to the west. A sergeant said they were going toward Spanish Town, the capital, to a place where the land was flat enough for a camp. Greg's first impression of Kingston was of a straight street lined with two-story houses, some with verandas in front, others with first-story roofs extending over the wooden sidewalk to form shaded arcades. Crowds of men, women and children, most of them black, stared curiously at the outlanders and gabbled comments in a soft odd accent that at first hearing was difficult to recognize as English.

The column crossed several streets at right angles and soon was

37

passing between lines of ramshackle huts and hovels. Beyond these the road became narrow and sandy between fields of tall, thickly-growing, long-leafed stalks. Sugar cane, Jed said, the chief crop of the island, and almost ready to be cut, crushed between rollers, and its juice boiled down and treated in various ways to make sugar or molasses or to be distilled into rum. Alternating with the fields of cane were groves of thin tall trees topped by fronds that made them look like feather dusters and bearing large pods. These were coconut palms, someone said, and the nuts had both juice and white meat inside. Here and there were tiny cottages, each surrounded by red, white and pink flowers. Truly it was a lush and fertile land they had come to.

At the steep bank of a small river the column turned left into an area dotted with huge trees, bigger than oaks, with tremendously thick trunks and wide-spreading branches that cast a welcome shade. Gratefully the men shed their equipment and sat down to wait for the tents and supplies.

"Most of a war is just waiting for what isn't where it should be when you want it," said Sergeant Simmons philosophically.

"And then it doesn't come after all," was Jed's knowledgeable contribution.

At Greg's question Jed identified the great trees as cotton trees. "'Bout the biggest tree on the island. Other places, some calls 'em kapoks an' some calls 'em ceibas. But it's all the same. Cotton trees they are, 'cause of the fluff in the pods."

After an hour's wait a courier on horseback appeared. The officers gathered around him, talked a few minutes, and then summoned the sergeants of the four companies.

Simmons was pensive when he returned. "The rest of the troops will be along shortly. So will the wagons, but they've got only tents. Captain Walker said nobody knows who's going to feed us. Virginia and the other colonies paid for the ships to get us here. England said she'd give us our rations and pay, but in Kingston they don't seem to know about that."

"Told you so," muttered Jed.

"Our governor's going to talk to the Jamaica governor and see what can be done. If he has to, ours will no doubt pay us out of his own credit, like he's been doing. Anyway, the Jamaica planters can't let us starve, and a lot of scrounging can be done, though like as not you'll get pretty tired of eating coconuts."

"Captain Walker says we're not to go beyond them low hills back there. Plantations farther back don't want to be disturbed and there's wild men beyond them, escaped slaves of the Spanish, most of them, called Maroons. Like nothing better than killing off strangers. Another thing, don't go trying to hack at these trees with any axes that may come along with the tents; we need the shade and the natives will haul down firewood from the hills."

This drew hollow laughter from the company.

"What's the use of firewood in this heat if we haven't got anything to cook?" demanded one.

"Fair question," conceded the sergeant. "For tonight we'll have rations—and firewood. Governor Gooch has already seen to that. It's what happens after tonight that matters."

"Reckon they'll feed the troops from England!" proclaimed a loud voice. The sergeant acted as if he had not heard.

It was bad news. It made Greg feel hungrier than he actually was. Perhaps Mr. Woodford would give him a meal when he delivered the letter. He would somehow get into Kingston as soon as possible. But no one was allowed away from camp until the tents were pitched, muskets cleaned and piled, and uniforms refurbished. That afternoon there came a solid downpour of rain that lasted a full hour, which, said Jed grumpily, was because it was the little rainy season, which would soon end.

The next morning the company was informed that their general, Governor Gooch, had arranged to buy provisions on credit in Kingston, thus temporarily solving the problem. Details from the various companies now present would be sent to town to carry back the purchases. From those of the company who volunteered, Sergeant Simpson picked 20 men. Greg, Jed and another of their tentmates named Sam Jenkins, who admired Jed, were among those chosen.

As the detail took the road to Kingston it mingled with other groups from the Virginia, Maryland, and Pennsylvania companies on the same errand. As they set out on the six mile walk, Greg noticed that in the detail from Captain Bushrod's company, which had pitched camp nearby, was the man named Vizer Bates, whom he had not seen since the companies had boarded ship separately in Virginia.

It was clear and not too hot, and beyond the hills they could occasionally catch glimpses of the blue peaks of the mountain ridge. Freedom to walk as they pleased was exhilarating, and the men kept passing up and down the line to talk to friends in other companies. One of these was Bates. A glance from his pale eyes flicked briefly at Greg, then he greeted Jed. "So you made it," he drawled.

Jed scowled and gave a grunt by way of reply.

"Still the same old cheery shipmate," smirked Bates, and passed on.

The procession rounded an arm of the great harbor and a half hour later sighted the first scraggly shacks outside Kingston.

"Who knows where I can find a mug of ale?" demanded one of the mean-faced ex-convicts. "They got taverns here?"

"Plenty of 'em," replied Jed. "Don't worry. One of them's called the *Sailfish*. It's by the wharves. No trouble there, except it takes money." The question of how and when they were going to be paid provided conversation for the next mile.

In the midst of it Greg turned to Jed. "I've got to deliver a message first," he said in a low voice, "but if I can find someone to show me the office of a man named Woodford, that shouldn't take long. Suppose I meet you at the *Sailfish* an hour after we get to town."

Jed nodded. Typically, if he was surprised he did not show it. "Be waiting for you. 'T'aint a big town."

As they came to the beginning of Port Royal Street the line of marchers broke up into groups seeking shelter from the sun under the occasional roofs over the sidewalks. A crowd of small ragged children began racing among them, shouting in their nearly-incomprehensible dialect.

"What they saying?" asked Sam Jenkins.

"Some's just begging money," Jed told him disgustedly. "Some wants to sell us fruit or show us where we can get a drink. Don't trust any of 'em." Again Jed was what he called facing facts.

At the intersection of a wide street Greg stepped out of his group, nodded to Jed, and began to consider how he would go about finding the office of Mr. Woodford. There were no street signs. Well, he'd have to ask.

Jed and Sam turned toward the waterfront. "We'll see you at the *Sailfish*," said Jed.

At that moment a small boy, his ragged pants held up by a green ribbon about his middle, darted from around a corner and ran to him.

"You want guide, sar? You want go some place? Yis, sar. My name Jacob. Bestest guide in Kingston." He was hopping up on one foot then the other, his whole face shining with eagerness.

"Yes," said Greg, answering the boy's wide grin. "I am looking for the office of Mr. Woodford on Prince Street."

"I take you there, sar. Mr. Woodford, he very well known merchant. I take you there now."

He skipped ahead and Greg followed him to a corner, down a side street, and around another corner. A country cart loaded with logs went by, then two barefoot women carrying huge bundles of white clothes on their heads. At the fifth house, which had a wide veranda on the second story, the boy leaped up the one step to the wooden porch and opened the door with a flourish.

"Visitor for Mr. Woodford," he called loudly and stood on one foot in the open door. Greg reached into his pocket. He knew he must give the boy something, but he had only a ha'penny and a shilling. He held out the ha'penny and the child grabbed it, looked at it, made grimace of anger and ran away.

Greg stepped into cool dimness. Streaks of sunlight from between the closed slatted blinds striped the dark polished floor. A man at a desk in the corner of the room said "Yes?" inquiringly.

"Is Mr. Woodford in " asked Greg eagerly. It would be good to have his mission accomplished. "I have a message for him."

"Message?" repeated the man.

"Yes, from Virginia."

The man gave him an odd look and paused thoughtfully. "I will tell Mr. Woodford," he said, rising and going quickly through a door at the back.

Greg seated himself in one of the two straight chairs. The office was very bare, even for a clerk. Greg waited for what seemed an excessive time. Why should it take so long? There was no sound of voices from the room beyond. He was taking a turn around the room when the door opened. "Mr. Woodford will see you now," said the clerk and stood aside for Greg to pass.

The inner office was equally dark and bare, with a desk planted in the middle. The man behind it wore a white shirt and the pale face above it was long and narrow with dark eyes.

"You say you have a message from Virginia?" he asked in a low but rasping voice.

This was a scene Greg had rehearsed in his mind. "The wind is from the north," he said quickly.

"It usually is at this time of day," replied the man irritably. "You may give me the message. It is from Pollock, I presume."

Greg kept his face impassive. Perhaps the merchant had forgotten the answer to the password, or had expected a different phrasing. He tried again. "The north wind is blowing."

"I have agreed," said the man coldly. "Now let me have the letter." One hand curled as it stretched out on the desk.

Something was decidedly wrong. "I—I don't have a letter," stammered Greg. "I just came to bring you his good wishes."

"Nonsense. You do have it. Carlos!"

At the sound of the door opening Greg whirled to grapple with the clerk, who was raising a knife. Greg seized the knife arm and twisted it. He had moved so quickly that the fellow was thrown off balance and fell to the floor. The other man leaped around the desk and seized Greg from behind, pinioning his arms. "Get his belt. Quick," he ordered the clerk who was scrambling to his feet and lunged at Greg's waist. Greg managed to kick him in the stomach, which doubled him for a moment.

The outer door was suddenly flung open and footsteps were coming across the floor. "Get out the grappling irons, Sam. It's time to board. Didn't believe the boy, but he was right to fetch us."

Never had a voice been so welcome as Jed's as he and Sam moved purposefully toward the man whose arms were still locked around Greg.

"Just a misunderstanding, men," said the cold voice, and the

arms loosened their grasp. "Carlos thought the young, er, soldier was about to attack me." The fellow was completely composed.

"Think up a better story next time." Jed's voice was filled with contempt. He looked at Greg. "Tried to knife you, I see. As I guess you've found out, this ain't your Mr. Woodford. Let's go." And the three marched out of the office, across the veranda to the street.

"Whew!" Greg stopped and wiped his forehead on his sleeve. "Thanks. But how'd you know?"

Jed leaned against a corner post. "I saw the boy that spoke to you. He come running up to me at the *Sailfish*. Knowed it was the same one 'count of the green ribbon 'round his middle. Said you had no money to give him for takin' you to that place an' had told him to come to me an' I'd give him a shilling. Must have heard me say I'd meet you at the *Sailfish* when he came up to you. Easy to see he's lying 'cause I knew you had one shilling and that's too much to give him, an' you knew I wouldn't give him a shilling on his say so. I said we'd come back an' ask you. So he brought us right here.

"I got to thinking as we walked an' asked him how come he spoke to you in the first place. He said a soldier on the street pointed you out to him, told him to take you to that place when you asked for Woodford's house, an' had given him a shilling to do it. He told the boy he was a friend of yours, an' that it was just a joke on you 'cause it wasn't Woodford's at all. All in fun, it was."

"Now, who . . . ?" began Greg.

Jacob was jumping up and down eagerly. "I tol' you. I took you there. See? A joke."

Greg pulled the coin from his pocket. Jacob skipped nearer. "Knew I'd get me another shilling," he crowed.

"Just a minute." Greg held the coin out of reach. "Who gave you money to take me to the wrong place and said it was a joke?"

"Don't know, sar," whined Jacob. "Never see him before. He in uniform like all the rest."

"What did he look like?"

"Can't say, sar. When I see his shilling I don't pay him much mind. Don't I get my shilling, sar?"

"Do you know the office of the real Mr. Woodford?"

"Oh, yis, sar."

"Then you take us there right now," interrupted Jed, seizing one of the boy's thin arms. "An' if it ain't the right place this time'stead of a shilling you'll get a whuppin' you won't forget."

Jacob nodded and beamed. "Oh. I take you to right place now, sars. No one paying me to do different."

"I don't know what this is about," growled Jed aside to Greg, "but one thing I'll wager, there's somebody among our own folk—unless this boy's lying again—who's out to do you harm."

"That may be," replied Greg in a low voice. "After we see Mr. Woodford I'll tell you all I know."

The house, just off Port Royal Street, was larger than the first house, with neatly kept bushes and a small lawn around it. The door was opened by a young clerk.

"I am looking for the office of Mr. James Woodford," said Greg firmly, as he stepped inside.

An elderly man came from behind a desk and peered at Greg over his square spectacles. "This is his place of business, but Mr. Woodford is not here today. May I be of assistance?"

Greg nodded at Jed and held out the shilling to Jacob, who grabbed it and raced for the street. "I must see Mr. Woodford," Greg went on. "Do you know where he is?"

"At his home outside the town. Often he stays there a day or so during the week to oversee his plantation."

"How do we find him?"

"It is a bit of a walk," was the reply. "Perhaps seven miles. You must take the road to the left at the end of the wharves, continue, going east, past the base of the peninsula that encloses the harbor. You continue east, rounding the end of Long Mountain, across a small river and on to a valley where you take a road to the left up a hillside. Mr. Woodford's place is a large stone house and the name *Bonaventure* is enscrolled in the iron gates."

"I've got to go there," Greg told Jed after they thanked the clerk and left. "I must get the letter to him, and tell him.—"

"Sure. I'll come with you. If there's to be more trouble two of us can handle it better than one."

So Sam rejoined the food detail for supplies for camp and Greg and Jed took the road out of town.

It was dusty and the heat had grown oppressive. Tall strange trees grew on either side, but neither they nor the occasional palms threw much shade on the road itself. They crossed the base of the peninsula that led to Port Royal and later a sturdy bridge raised high above the stream below, and at last turned up a hillside. Here they could look down on a river valley with cultivated plots, and, to their right, glimpse the mouth of the river and the blue sea beyond. As they walked Greg told Jed about Mr. Pollock's message to the merchant of Kingston.

Finally they came to two gray stone pillars and between them an open iron gate bearing the name *Bonaventure*. Beyond, a driveway curved around some gay flower beds and ended at a terrace in front of a house built of massive stone blocks. Two stories high, with square towers at each corner, it looked solid and impregnable. Long windows faced the terrace from either side of a heavy door set in a massive stone framework. Jed pointed out that the windows had outside shutters of wood thick enough to withstand bullets. A white-clad servant came to the open door as the two mounted the steps to the terrace. On being told that they wished to see Mr. Woodford he led them to a large, high-ceilinged room on the left that overlooked the beach and the sea.

The man who rose from a desk to greet them was slender and gray-haired, with humorous brown eyes and a ready smile.

"Mr. Woodford?" asked Greg. Here was indeed a man he could trust; he was sure this was the right man at last.

"Yes." He shook hands quickly, and though his glance seemed casual, Greg was sure he had noticed everything about them.

"I've come from Virginia," Greg began.

If the other was surprised he did not show it, but motioned them to chairs. "After the walk from town you must be dry," he smiled and nodded to the servant who disappeared. "You must try our orange juice; it is very refreshing. Then I hope you will stay for dinner, which is at two."

Jed looked pleased and relieved at the invitation. The orange drink was indeed delicious. Greg drained his glass and set it down, anxious to tell this friendly man all that had happened. But first . . . "The wind seems to be from the north," he remarked casually.

"But soon it will be from the east and then the south," replied the other gravely, then smiled. "Yes. You are right; one must make sure in these matters. You come from Mr. Pollock. Tell me of my friend-by-letter in Williamsburg and what has brought you here."

Greg told of his commission, then, unfastening his money belt, took out the sealed letter and handed it across the desk. Next he told of what had happened that morning while Mr. Woodford listened impassively.

When he had finished Mr. Woodford brought from the pocket of his jacket a crumpled piece of paper. "I am surprised, and yet not surprised. This is the reason I am at *Bonaventure* today."

On the paper he handed Greg was scrawled: "i will cum to yur house with litre from Mr. P."

"This was delivered to my office yesterday. Now that I see you I realize this is not how you would write, but," he spread his hands, "how could I tell? So I stayed." He paused, staring thoughtfully out of the window.

"A house alongside an alleyway, a bare dark office? Then I know. It is the house and office of a rival in trade, almost an enemy, if I permitted him that importance. A man who calls himself Walter Quinzaine and claims to be English but probably is French or Spanish. He is in league with several pirates, or privateers as they call themselves now, and will go to any lengths to learn of merchant ships, when they sail and their goods. He and a bucko named Coutts have had some success at their lawless game, which makes them avid for more. Now, excuse me, I will read this." He broke open the letter.

While the merchant read Greg gazed admiringly around the room. It was paneled to the ceiling with the same handsome, polished reddish wood as the chairs, tables, and desk. Soft green draperies, swaying gently at the open windows, framed a view of the shore that was magnificent. Woven rugs of the same shade partly covered the gleaming floor. All this seemed lost on Jed, whose unblinking eyes were fixed on the merchant.

"Yes," said Mr. Woodford, placing the letter in a drawer. "This is most interesting and the business can be arranged. I thank you for bringing it. Now, in spite of your walk, we might take a short stroll outside as we wait for dinner. You may be interested in seeing more of the house."

Bonaventure was massive, not only in front but on every side. "It needs to be," Mr. Woodford explained. "The pirates in the old days often attacked and pillaged plantation houses, and the privateers do also, occasionally, though they have to be more cautious about it these days. Also, there are bands of former slaves, outlaws, back in the mountains, but you have probably heard of the Maroons, who come down on isolated houses to kill and rob. By their very nature, most plantation houses are isolated. You see no bushes or small trees are allowed to grow near the house, and those large trees, allspice and mahogany, and the palms, are kept at a distance. Life can be pleasant here in Jamaica, but also dangerous, for there are the fevers and plagues that somehow reach us. That is why I sent my wife and children back to England six months ago. I hope, in a year or two, to follow them, at least for a while."

From the house came two notes of a horn. "Ah, that is dinner."

The dining room was to their right as they entered the central hall. A table covered with white linen and laid with porcelain and silverware awaited them. Over a meal of strange dishes, of which Greg recognized only roast pork, Mr. Woodford questioned them about Virginia, the voyage, the camp. At news of the shortage of food at Hunt's Bay he frowned. "That is disturbing, that soldiers, who have come to fight for us should not have proper stores. I will speak to some of my friends. Tomorrow Governor Trelawney is giving a dinner for your Governor Gooch in Spanish Town. I will also talk to them."

As they were about to leave for the long walk back to camp Mr. Woodford beckoned to a tall, very black man with a broad face and bright, intelligent eyes. "This is Stanley," the merchant said, "my trusted bodyguard and assistant. You, in turn, may trust him whenever I send him to you. I will tell him of your adventure, Greg, but I do not think you will be troubled again for Quinzaine will know I have the letter now. I will see you soon." He shook hands formally and returned to the house.

"That's a right nice man," said Jed heartily as they started down the driveway. "And he sets a mighty good table. That meal will last me till tomorrow, for sure."

FIVE

Governor Gooch's American Regiment

Mr. Woodford did indeed speak to Governor Trelawney and Governor Gooch and some planter friends, for three days later Greg was summoned to the house on the road to Spanish Town where the Governor had set up headquarters. He was sitting in the shade of a great cotton tree puffing on his clay pipe. His eyes twinkled as Greg smartly saluted.

"You have a good friend in James Woodford, Shelby," he observed, "and thanks to you I believe the troops have also. What ever fumbling has gone on in London, he and Governor Trelawney are trying to put all to rights. He has requested that you and two others come to stay at his plantation so that you may each third day escort a cart of meat, fruit and vegetables he will gather from his own place and those of his friends to help with our commissary. Governor Trelawney has promised similar aid, and if we can purchase some cattle our men may get at least two meals a day. I have given my permission for your sojourn at the plantation. I envy you getting out of this heat."

He seized a palm leaf fan from the table beside him and fanned his face energetically. "This does not help, but creates an illusion,

49

but, at that, I prefer land and heat to the sea, eh, Shelby?" He smiled suddenly and Greg again understood why he was so popular.

With Jed and Sam, Greg moved to *Bonaventure,* its breezes, bountiful meals, and friendly host. The merchant rode in to Kingston almost every day and often stayed overnight at his town house. Every third day the three escorted one or two wagons to the camp of the colonials. Jed, refusing to ride a horse, sat beside the Negro driver and listened to lengthy accounts of life on the island, while Sam and Greg rode on either side.

On their second trip they saw a squadron of ships at anchor off Kingston and knew that Admiral Vernon had returned from cruising.

"That's the *Carolina,* the Admiral's flag ship." Jed pointed to one of the largest vessels. "He's brought the ships in close so's to leave room for the fleet from England. Under our present circumstances, I ain't in no hurry for it to come."

The Admiral's return had not, however, solved the problem of supplies for the Americans, as they learned at camp. Indeed, the situation was worse than ever because a large contingent of militiamen from New York and New England had just arrived, more than doubling the present size of the force known as Gooch's American Regiment. With them was the Adjutant General, an elderly Irishman named William Blakeney, with the rank of Colonel. When he found that the Admiral had only provisions for his own sailors, the Colonel set about energetically trying to increase the collection of food from the countryside, but without enough success.

After supper, on evenings when Mr. Woodford was at the plantation, he would talk to Greg of many things as they strolled on the terrace or, if the sea wind was strong, sat in the living room. Books and history were his favorite subjects at first, but gradually he came to tell of his home and life in England and of his wife and two daughters, whom he deeply missed. Once Greg asked him who had built *Bonaventure,* for it was evidently at least fifty years old.

Mr. Woodford lighted his pipe and settled into his chair. "The house goes back to the time of Henry Morgan, the pirate who was knighted and became governor. If I had realized the problems connected with the place I might not have bought it. It is not too far from the shore—though a steep climb—for an attack from the sea, and does not have the shelter of the harbor. Moreover, the plantation is laid out in several sections, some of them quite distant.

"While we now live in relatively peaceful times," he continued, "as far as buccaneers are concerned, this house is of special interest to a few successors of the Brethren of the Coast. It was built by one of Morgan's captains who brought away great loot from the sack of Panama and also captured many Spanish ships. This captain called himself Greengold, which undoubtedly was not his name, to proclaim to one and all that his only interest was in the green of emeralds from the mines of New Granada and gold from any source. Oddly enough, he was a good planter. He would gamble for emeralds and purchase any brought to him. He was said to have pounds of excellent stones."

Gold! Emeralds! That was the stuff of loot!

"Go on, sir," urged Greg. "What happened?"

"Twice men came to take this fortune from him, but his house, as you have seen, is built like a fort, and with his own fierce followers he beat off the raiders. After a time he died, quite peacefully, of some sort of a seizure. It was said he tried and tried to speak at the end, for he had the delusion the place was being attacked and kept pointing to the great hall entrance, which vastly amused his henchmen. As soon as he was dead his slaves decamped to the hills and his men practically took the house apart looking for the cache of jewels. They couldn't find it. It never has been found."

Greg sighed. " 'Tis a pity," he said wistfully.

"There have been rumors, started I doubt not by Quinzaine, among others, that I have found the jewels and have been selling them discreetly." Mr. Woodford smiled wryly. "I wish it were true—my fortune would be made."

"What could he have been pointing to?" asked Greg eagerly. "Have you looked both inside and outside the house?"

"Who wouldn't, my boy? Yes, I have looked occasionally, and others have before me. But I am not one to believe in fairy tales. This is all supposition founded upon a legend. There is nothing behind these panels, for I had them installed myself to cover the stone walls. The treasure, if it exists, could be anywhere. Likely enough it is buried somewhere on the grounds, and the way vegetation grows here it could quickly be covered and hidden forever. But desperate men still hope. Even in my time here there was a raid by a boatload of men shouting they had come for the Greengold treasure. Luckily enough, servants sleep in the house and they can handle guns. A few shots from them drove off the brigands. Always since then I have kept a sentinel in one of the towers, day and night."

"The pointing," mused Greg. "It must have meant something. Do you know where he was when he had the seizure?"

"Why, in this room, I believe. He was quarreling with one of his men. But," he said, shrugging. "It is futile to speculate."

"I suppose so," Greg agreed sadly. "But it is a fine tale."

It had not been possible to write letters on the ship or at the camp, but now, in the spacious coolness of the room at *Bonaventure,* Greg spent a day trying to describe the voyage and the sights and ways of this strange island for his mother and father. Mr. Woodford promised to send the letter by the first trustworthy captain heading for any Virginia port.

Each third day when the three companions arrived at the camp they found it in a more unhappy state. In spite of the contributions and the best efforts of Governor Trelawney and Colonel Blakeney, food was scarce. Some men were down with fevers. There was no one to care for them and they could only trust to their comrades to bring them water and what food they could eat. Openly angry at the colonies and the British government for their neglect, the soldiers who were well did the minimum of required drill and spent their time off roaming the countryside looking for odd jobs to earn a few pence or robbing orchards or killing half-wild pigs in the woods for meat. It was no wonder that the men who crowded around the plantation wagons while the sergeants doled out the supplies muttered among themselves.

"You three have it mighty easy up there in the hills," said one. "We all better move up with you and that fancy gent."

"Shut up," commanded Sergeant Simmons. "If it wasn't for them you wouldn't be holding that yam in your fist, Rawlings. You learn to be thankful for what you get in the army and not question where it comes from. That's why I'm not asking you where you got that chicken yesterday."

With the arrival of four North Carolina companies and, some days later, a final contingent from the northern colonies, the American force of 3,500 was complete. Toward the middle of December Governor Gooch ordered all who were fit for duty to Spanish Town to be reviewed there by Governor Trelawney of Jamaica and Admiral Vernon. Greg, who was in camp at the time, guessed the parade was as much to tighten discipline and give the men a workout as it was to show them off.

The capital was smaller than Kingston and well inland. Its streets were laid at right angles and in the meaner parts the small houses crowded close to the roads, but the homes of the wealthy were set back amid towering trees and blooming vines and shrubs. Some of the houses appeared to have been built in Spanish times, before the British took Jamaica.

The troops marched to the square in the center of town where, drawn up in closed ranks, they were inspected with a formality that made many stir uneasily and welcome the order "At ease." The Governor and the Admiral each made a short speech, the Governor's somewhat ponderous, the Admiral's incisive but friendly.

Greg admired Vernon immediately. He was a stately figure, with his epaulets and uniform a-shine with gold braid. The dark eyes in the oblong face looked amused and the chin and mouth were firm. Recently the nickname "Old Grog" had been given him because of a cloak of grosgrain cloth, a mixture of coarse silk, mohair, and wool, which he often wore. From this had come "grog" as the name of a drink he had decreed throughout his fleet. During the previous August, while cruising under the blazing sun of the Caribbean, he had ordered that the tot of raw rum issued twice daily to sailors be diluted by mixing a half pint of rum with a quart of water. Raw rum, he had said, might warm a man's insides in cold northern waters, but it was no stuff to drink in the tropics. To everyone's surprise but his own, the health and efficiency of the sailors had immediately improved, and now even the sailors had come around to his point of view.

The spirits of the colonials rose somewhat when early in January a grand fleet, now overdue, appeared at the harbor mouth and, to the faintly heard booms of saluting cannon from the fort at Port Royal, sailed, ship after ship, into the great bay. It was the fleet from England under Sir Chaloner Ogle, who was to be second in command to Admiral Vernon. Far outnumbering the Admiral's squadron, it had twenty-seven ships of the line and many smaller vessels, one hundred and seventy sails in all, said to be manned by thirteen thousand sailors and carrying in transports nine thousand British regulars and six hundred marines. It was the largest concentration of naval power ever sent by Britain into Caribbean waters. Even this armada did not fill the bay between Port Royal and Kingston.

Sailors and smartly uniformed soldiers soon crowded the streets of the towns. The colonials eyed them in silence, feeling little in common with them. These men were professionals—fed and paid. Nevertheless, Jed found an old friend, now in the Thirty-fifth Regiment, impressively uniformed in a long red coat with yellow-faced skirts tied back at each side from knees to waist, black tricorn hat, short red breeches above long white buttoned gaiters and low black shoes. When Jed reported it took nigh half a day to keep the uniform spotless Greg and Sam felt better about their own more simple and less ornamented outfit, which was enough trouble. Jed began going off with his friend, mingling with the British, and coming back with news.

"General Cathcart, him that was a lord and commander of the army, went an' died on the way out," he reported after his first round. "Whole army says that's bad. He was a real soldier. Served with Marlborough, same as your Governor."

"Who's the commander now?" asked Sam.

"Name of Wentworth. Good at drill an' spit an' polish, too good, they say. Elsewise they don't know much about him 'cause he's never commanded on his own in a real war. If I'm going to fight I want under a man who knows his job."

"Well, Admiral Vernon does," put in Greg. "Maybe this new general does, too."

Jed shook his head. "If he don't, Admiral can't give him

orders—independent commands, see? We just got to hope," he added pessimistically. "We better get back to the plantation and collect a lot of grub. Something tells me you Americans are going to be kind of restive, way things are going."

One evening when Mr. Woodford returned from Kingston he was silent and preoccupied during supper, ate little, and when it was over quickly went outside and began pacing up and down the terrace. Sam was back in camp and Jed was in his own room. Greg was reading when Stanley touched him on the shoulder.

"You go out talk to Massa Woodford. He in some kind of trouble. Might do him good to talk about it."

Surprised, Greg arose, entered the hall and went to the great door opening on the terrace. There he hesitated. Mr. Woodford was still pacing, hands clasped behind his back, head bent. Greg wondered if it would be impertinent for him to interrupt. But Stanley knew his master well, perhaps it really would do him good to talk. So Greg fell into step beside the dim figure.

"Has something gone wrong, sir?" he asked hesitantly. "Can I do anything to help "

Mr. Woodford put his hand on Greg's arm. "Thank you, my boy. There is nothing anyone can do at the moment."

"Would you care to tell me . . . ?" began Greg.

"It seems," interrupted the other, and his voice was calm, "that I have underestimated Quinzaine. Ten nights ago my office was broken into and my desk pried open. Most of the papers there were of no particular value, with one exception. I had left for final checking a copy of my sailing orders for my sloop Nancy and the manifest of the cargo. She had sailed that morning for Hampton Roads, New York, and London. I was disturbed at the breaking in, but not unduly. I supposed the thieves were after money."

He paused, took a deep breath, and continued. "Today Captain Richards and his crew returned. He told me the Nancy had been run down in the channel between Cuba and Hispaniola by a barque commanded by the man who calls himself Captain Coutts, the rapacious privateer who is in alliance with Quinzaine, who knew exactly where to find her. Richards is a good man and put up a fight, but when the *Nancy's* mainmast was shot away he could do nothing more. The cargo was transferred—and the barque vanished. Richards managed a makeshift jury rig and limped back to port. He at least saved the vessel, but the loss of the cargo is a blow."

"Can't you go to the Governor, go after Coutts?" asked Greg, aghast.

Mr. Woodford seemed to shrug. "The Governor, and all this grand flotilla, are occupied with the invasion. It will be almost impossible to find Coutts now, and he will be avoiding Jamaica for a while. If and when he does return I could swear out a warrant and probably have him arrested and held for trial. But Richards and the crew would have to be on hand to testify. All that is in the problematical future. No. I must refit the *Nancy* and try again. But the loss is—distressing."

He suddenly put an arm around Greg's shoulder. "I am glad to have talked thus with you. It has helped to clarify the problem, as speaking aloud to a sympathetic friend so often does."

The next morning Mr. Woodford was his usual pleasant self, but he spent more nights in town and Greg and Jed missed him.

When, late in January, it was rumored that the army would soon be sailing, they were ordered by Captain Walker to return to camp. Now that he was there for more than brief visits, Greg was appalled at the condition of the American troops. Sickness and discontent were increasing daily. One day after morning drill a knot of men gathered in the street of a New York company. They were soon joined by troops of other colonies, all arguing and gesticulating.

News of what was happening quickly spread throughout the American regiment. Greg and Jed joined the others running from all directions.

"The British get three meals a day," a soldier was shouting. "Three meals! What do we get? Where's our rations?"

"Rations. Rations," chorused some men excitedly. "We're being cheated. They promised us grub."

A sergeant from New England was hoisted up by two men. "Silence," he bellowed. "Behave like soldiers."

"Shut your mouth," a voice shouted. "Some couldn't be soldiers no how, like New York wharf rats," yelled another. "No cod eater can call me that," was a shouted reply. And a fight began.

Normally the men from the different colonies were tolerant of each other's strange accents and ways, but now, goaded to fury by their treatment, the differences were fanning their anger. Fights were breaking out all over the field.

Above the clamor Greg heard the sound of drumbeats from the direction of Spanish Town. He turned and saw Governor Gooch, with a group of officers following him, spurring to the scene. Behind them came a company of British troops led by General Wentworth.

Gooch rode his horse into the midst of the milling throng and rose in his stirrups. "Stop this," he roared in a voice that he probably had not used since he campaigned with Marlborough. "Come to attention!"

Those near him heard and obeyed, and gradually the flailing fists were lowered and the men turned sullenly toward the impressive figure.

"What is the meaning of this disturbance?" shouted Gooch. "Can't I trust you to behave yourselves while I hold a conference with the officers of this regiment?"

By this time the drumming had stopped, but the British company led by Wentworth, followed by another, came smartly on until they were halted near the mob of Americans. Wentworth's face was white. He seemed horrified.

"Now," Gooch shouted as the clamoring voices stilled. "What is the matter with you?"

The answer came from many voices. "Rations. Food. We want regular rations. We don't get none."

Gooch looked troubled and his own voice lowered a little. "I know it. I have done what I could. I'm told it will be changed."

"General Gooch, sir." A tall New Englander stepped forward, unabashed, and saluted. "We all come gladly, or most of us did, when we was told we was needed to fight the Spanish. But a man can't fight on a few cups of muddy water and one sweet potato a day. He can't hardly live. 'Taint right to ask it."

Another, hatchet-faced and serious, moved up beside him.

"That's right, sir. Them," jerking a thumb toward the regulars, "gits fed right and proper."

"That proclamation from the King, God bless him, said we'd git fed like the soljers from England," called out a voice.

"Why ain't he done it?" demanded another. "He's lied to us."

At this Wentworth, looking even more shocked, cried out shrilly, "General Gooch, this is insubordination!"

The Governor turned to him calmly. "Perhaps it is, sir. But they have a just grievance. I trust matters will be set right when we board ship."

"We ain't against you, Governor." This time it was a Virginian, speaking kindly. "We know you've done your best. It's England that's not done right by us."

"This is mutiny!" shouted Wentworth in a fury.

"Calm down now, men," ordered Gooch, loudly. "Get back to your companies. Whatever can be done for you will be done. Don't disgrace your colonies. I am going to review this regiment in half an hour. Be ready to turn out then."

Miraculously, it worked. The Americans dispersed as ordered. General Wentworth, still enraged, turned his column of regulars around and began the march toward Spanish Town. The review was held and a crisis was averted. But for the British "undisciplined" became an adjective attached to the Americans, and it stuck.

Not long after this incident, Stanley, delivering a wagonload of provisions, sought out Greg with word that Mr. Woodford would like to see him at his house in Kingston. Greg secured overnight leave and rode back in the wagon. He wondered why Stanley, who usually would answer questions and talk about the island if encouraged, had so little to say.

It was early dusk when they arrived, the moon would rise soon. The house, set back a little from the street and surrounded by trees and shrubs, was square and white, with verandas on three sides of the two stories. Stanley showed him into a large room on the first floor. In the dimness he did not see the figure on the chaise longue until Mr. Woodford called his name.

"Welcome. Come sit here beside me," said the merchant, gesturing to an armchair by a small table. He was wearing a dressing gown over a nightshirt and a light blanket covered his knees. His right arm was in a sling.

"What has happened, sir?" asked Greg anxiously. "Are you ill?"

Mr. Woodford smiled faintly. "No. Just disabled. Another attempt at robbery. An order of silver, a handsome set, had arrived from England and I had it brought here for safekeeping until I could arrange for its delivery. I had gone to bed, but the wind kept me awake. I thought I heard a sound on the veranda and then, a little later, another from this room. A sneak thief, I thought, and seized my heavy walking stick and came down quietly. At first I saw nothing, but then by the dim glow of moonlight showing through the window, I perceived two figures carrying boxes. I shouted for Stanley and rushed at them with my stick.

"I caught one on the side of the head with my first blow." There was satisfaction in the quiet voice. "He went down. The other dropped his box and jumped at me from the side. I was not quick enough in turning and he stabbed me in the shoulder. As I tried to corner him he shoved a chair at me; it caught me off-balance, I tripped over it and fell—breaking my leg. By this time Stanley was on hand and the man fled, leaving his stunned companion, and my boxes. The accomplice turned out to be a petty thief who claimed he had been hired to move some goods and did not know the man with him or where the boxes were to go. There was no further lead, but I have my suspicions. Be that as it may, the thing is that I am laid up, for it happened only two nights ago. I cannot use my arm and the surgeon has bound me in splints and I cannot walk. He assures me the break is clean and I will walk well again in three months or so."

"If I had known I would have come," cried Greg. "Is there anything I can do for you?"

"Yes, Greg. I have decided after long thought that there is. But, first, I am glad to tell you I believe I have taken care of Mr. Pollock; a brig sailed yesterday with a cargo for him, which should ease his situation. With that off my mind, I felt free to attend to a matter of my own, to go on a voyage myself, a voyage of great importance to me. Now that I am house bound, I am going to ask you to do an errand for me."

"Anything, gladly. You know that, sir."

"Thank you, but wait. You are not to run into any danger on my behalf; if that seems likely you are to abandon it all.

'Now, as you know, I have had severe losses lately. A means of replacing them and setting my business on firm ground, has come to hand in the form of a very large commission from my London merchant for a collection of emeralds from Cartagena, for some "noble person," as he put it. Cartagena is the best place in the world for emeralds, for they are mined in the mountains of New Granada. I planned to go in my own schooner, get there ahead of the British fleet and lie at a distance from the city, and then get in touch with a merchant there whom I met once and with whom I have dealt. He would buy the stones on a commission and deliver them to me at the place where I would wait, and I would then return with the jewels. But now. . . ."

His voice trailed off as a servant quietly entered the room, lighted the candles, and left. Mr. Woodford continued.

"Because of the war and the generally unsettled conditions, the demand for emeralds from the Spanish Main has risen and also the prices. My own commission would be substantial. Now, since I cannot go before our fleet lays siege to the city, it is my hope that you will be willing to carry a message from me to this merchant. I will see that the gems are brought back here. It is the message only for which I need you. Will you take it?"

"Of course, sir, and gladly, if I get any chance to land before the siege, or to find him later. But how will I find him?"

"I will tell you in a moment. Now, we are going to besiege Cartagena with such a powerful force there should be little doubt of the outcome. If the navy and army move quickly enough the place should be in our hands in a month, or less, after we arrive. But I dare not wait for the city to fall; it might be burned, looted, and the stocks of emeralds dispersed. So, I am asking you to find, if possible, the country house of this merchant, whose name is Charles Ogden, deliver my message and get him started on the job.

"His country place is well outside the city on a hill overlooking the great harbor, not far from the house of the South Sea factor. Ogden apparently is in very good standing with the Spanish authorities, or they would not let him do business there. I think he should be at the country place both because of our attack and the approach of the rainy season when the well-to-do move out to the hills to escape fevers. So much depends on this that it is worth taking the chance. I have racked my brains, but I can think of no other way of reaching him. Now, you must have a credential. Here is my signet ring. He will know it, for he has seen it and I use it as my seal."

Greg put the heavy ring on the third finger of his right hand where it fitted snugly. "Good," approved the other. "Find Ogden and tell him I will need a hundred good emeralds of varying sizes to be made into an elaborate necklace, a coronet, bracelets, a ring, and earrings. He is experienced, more than I in jewels, and will know the types of stones to get."

A gust of wind swept through the room and Mr. Woodford, as if conscious of the open windows, lowered his voice.

"Here is my plan. Any ship from Cartagena with dispatches for England will stop here on the way. When the first one brings news of the capture of the city, or even of the forcing of the forts that protect the harbor, I will send my schooner across. It will go to a bay called Bahia de Barbacoas, which is at the south end of a channel connecting that bay with the harbor of Cartagena. The channel is called the Paso Caballos and is used by the country people. The bay is used in the sloop trade, to evade the guarda-costas; small ships go unnoticed. We have been there before. Tell Ogden my ship will arrive within eight days after news reaches Kingston and will wait there for him." He paused and gave a little chuckle. "It is all a gamble—that somehow in the midst of a war you will be able to reach Ogden—that he will be able to find the emeralds—and that he will get them to the schooner. Even a staid merchant must take a chance and trust to luck once in a while. I only regret I cannot go myself."

"Yes, sir," said Greg, proud at being trusted with this important and daring mission. "But how do I find the house?"

"Here," smiled Mr. Woodford, pulling a folded paper from his pocket, "is a map I have drawn of Cartagena harbor as I remember it. This," he pointed to some crossed lines, "is the walled city facing the open sea. It is protected by rocks and shoals so that large ships cannot approach it closely enough to bombard it effectively. So it must be taken from the rear, as the Frenchman, de Pointis, did over forty years ago, by landing at this small inner harbor behind the city and its island suburb. Do you see?"

Greg nodded, his eyes on the map.

"This irregular oval is the main harbor, about ten miles long, almost an inland lake. There is only one entrance for ships, the Boca Chica, or little mouth, this narrow passage, which lies between this large triangular peninsula and the narrow long peninsula opposite. The large one is called Tierra Bomba. The Boca Chica is guarded by two small forts on the outer shore, a larger one on a hill facing the strait, and two others on the opposite point. Once these are all taken, the fleet can dispose of several minor forts in the harbor and the army can land behind the city.

"Now, here, across the harbor and opposite this point of Tierra Bomba, which juts eastward into the harbor, are some hills rising back from the shore. Halfway up one of these hills is the country house of Ogden. His estate lies above the road that follows the eastern side of the harbor from the Paso Caballos to the city, and near a creek running in, here. Follow a driveway from the road when you come to a sign that says *Hermosa*. That will lead you to identify the house. It should not be hard to find, once you are ashore in that area. Keep this map in your belt. Tell Mr. Ogden the schooner awaiting him is the *Agatha*; he knows it, and Captain McKestrick. One more thing; I hope you will take Jed into your confidence. In this sort of venture he could be helpful; he is a man of parts. Lastly, again, better the whole venture should fail than you should come to harm."

Suddenly Stanley's voice shouted from the darkness outside, "I see you, man. Don't try to get away."

There came a sound of scrabbling and crashing in the bushes and of two pairs of feet running up the street. His head bent a little, Mr. Woodford listened, tight-jawed. After a moment he passed a hand across his eyes. "Another try by Quinzaine, no doubt."

When Stanley returned from his chase he was apologetic. "I watched outside, sir, like you order," he panted. "He must have been already hid in the bushes. Only when bush stir do I spot him. But he a very fast man who duck into corners and around houses. I lose him. Too dark to see who he is. Very sorry, sir."

"No matter," Mr. Woodford told him grimly. "You did your best. Thank you. Perhaps he did not hear anything important." To Greg he added, "This may mean an element of danger. I had not expected it. Or I may be anticipating trouble where there is none. But, anyway, be careful. Now, tell me what news you hear of the expedition."

SIX

Action at Boca Chica

UNKNOWN to Greg, a council of war held at Spanish Town had decided to learn the intentions of a French fleet, now off Hispaniola, which Sir Chaloner Ogle's fleet had encountered on its way to Jamaica. Admiral Vernon could not sail for Cartagena leaving behind a flotilla that might either join the Spaniards or descend on Jamaica in his absence. The sloop of war *Wolfe*, which had escorted Gooch's transports to Jamaica, had been sent ahead to keep watch on the French.

Late in January the fleet began sailing in three sections from Port Royal, with the Americans scattered among thirty-five of the ships because there seemed no way to feed them other than to let them have shares of the British rations. When Greg learned that Captain Lawrence Washington's company was to be aboard Admiral Vernon's *Carolina* he rather envied them until he found his own company, under Captain Walker, would be on the same ship of the line as Governor Gooch. This was the *Hampton Court*, captained by Sir Digby Dent. The whole force sailed for Cape Tiburon on the tip of Hispaniola.

At Tiburon the *Wolfe* turned up with a French sloop whose captain set Admiral Vernon's mind at rest. Because of the nearness of the rainy season and an outbreak of sickness, the French fleet had returned home leaving only one ship and some merchantmen at nearby Port Louis. There was a delay of two weeks or more while the British fleet re-stocked wood and fresh water. At long last, in

65

late February, the Admiral sailed, sending two sloops ahead to sound a bay between Punta Canoa and Cartagena for safe anchorage.

A ship of the line was quite different from a transport, Greg discovered as he wandered wherever he was allowed around the decks. The ship had 80 guns on its several gun decks; its poop towered high above the water at the stern, and it had a crew of some 500, two thirds of them to serve the guns. The sailors chattered among themselves but held rather aloof from the Americans. With the torrid heat, foul air between decks and scanty, ill-cooked food, it was no wonder so many of the soldiers fell ill.

Ten days after leaving Tiburon the fleet reached Punta Canoa but the anchorage was a bad one, with shoals and little protection from stormy winds. After a council of war of the chief officers of the army and navy to settle how the future plunder was to be divided, General Wentworth and some of his officers boarded the man of war *Lion* to reconnoitre the coast and town a few miles to the south. Another council of war agreed to send three eighty-gun ships to batter the small forts of San Felipe and San Iago on the seaward side of Tierra Bomba, the outer guardians of the Boca Chica passage to the harbor. All this took time, but on the morning of March 9th the fleet sailed down the coast to Boca Chica.

Trying to keep out of the way of the sailors, Greg and Jed crouched behind a gunwale and peered at the low green coast as the *Hampton Court*'s bow rose and fell with the swell.

"We'll be sighting Cartagena pretty soon," observed Jed.

As the great gray walls of the city rose from the sea the ships swung out from shore to avoid the rocks and shoals that protected it from attack. The sudden thud of a cannon shot made Greg jump.

"Warning us off," commented Jed, as the shot hit the water far short of the ship. "Just wasting a cannon ball."

Greg gazed with wonder at this, the first city completely enclosed by walls he had ever seen. The walls and the several formidable forts rising from them were so massive they gave the impression they had been there since time began. Within the walls rose the double towers of a big church. Beyond the city, on the mainland, was a hill crowned by a fort, and still farther inland a higher hill with a building of some sort on its summit. There was another boom and again Greg jumped.

"You'll get so used to that you won't notice it," Jed told him. "Looks like we got to do the thing the hard way and take each fort one by one. And that's no way to make a living."

"Why'd you choose it?" Greg asked suddenly. He had never felt before he could ask Jed a personal question. Perhaps it was the faint sound of cannonading ahead, where the ships were bombarding the smaller forts and batteries on the coast, that led him to it.

The bright brown eyes looked at him levelly from the thin face. "Like to eat," Jed answered matter-of-factly. "Big family. No food. Got knocked around each day when I couldn't bring back a copper. Ran away and found I couldn't earn a ha'penny. Nothing to do but enlist, and keep coming back when time's up."

Greg felt a rush of admiration and affection for this thin little man and his acceptance of a hard life, but he could think of nothing to say. He nodded and looked toward the green-forested peninsula. He hoped it would not take long to reach Mr. Ogden and that they all would, somehow, return soon to Jamaica.

But it was all to take longer than anyone expected, with delay piling on delay.

The British bombardment of the two shore forts facing the sea stopped in late afternoon as the ships which then arrived anchored nearby. The Spaniards had abandoned the works and batteries on the shore and retreated through the woods of Tierra Bomba to the main fort of Boca Chica, which overlooked and guarded the narrow passage into the harbor. Along with several Spanish ships anchored in that passage, it continued to exchange cannon shots with the nearer British vessels. Signals flew from ship to ship to make ready for a landing. Then some more time was lost, for no apparent reason, in collecting boats for the grenadiers who were to go ashore. Before sundown, however, the first contingent landed.

At this point General Wentworth began to show his fatal indecision. Signals from his ship recalled the grenadiers to their barges after they had landed, and the barges were then ordered to lie off shore until reinforcements could be gathered. This maneuver puzzled all who watched. It was dark when the additional troops were

finally embarked and both forces went ashore to take possession of forts found to be abandoned. By then a rising surf prevented further troop landings.

In the morning General Wentworth joined the soldiers and during the next three days a large number of troops and quantities of supplies were ferried to land. A camp was laid out, tents were pitched by a Jamaican contingent and work was begun on a gun platform to bombard Castillo Boca Chica.

At first it appeared that no Americans were to be put ashore, but later came word that three hundred of them, from several ships, would be landed. Greg privately believed that Governor Gooch had made strong representations to Vernon and Wentworth, otherwise none would have been allowed to join the regulars. The Americans from the *Hampton Court* were among those chosen, and Gooch was in the first boatload.

To their surprise, the men found that little had been accomplished. Over-cautious, fearful of a Spanish attack, General Wentworth had kept his men under arms day and night. So many were being used as guards at posts scattered through the woods that much of the labor on the gun platform and camp had been left to the Jamaicans and sailors borrowed from the fleet. Wentworth seemed to think he had all the time in the world as he set about methodically planning a formal siege. He ordered one British regiment and the Americans to begin cutting fascines and pickets— wooden rods and stakes used to face and support earthworks. When the Americans learned that he wanted 50,000 fascines and 40,000 pickets they began to doubt his sanity.

All began to have the same doubts concerning the chief engineer. He had set some of the Jamaicans and sailors to work digging a trench through the stony soil in the direction of the fort, and others to constructing an elaborate gun platform behind a small rocky slope. The camp was being pitched directly between the gun platform and the shore. The platform itself seemed fairly open to enemy fire in spite of the ridge, but the engineer apparently did not consider it necessary to dig connecting trenches to it for the protection of artillerymen entering or leaving it.

While cutting fascines in the woods of Tierra Bomba the Americans occasionally could get a clear view of the fort. Built of stone, it was an irregular square, about 360 feet to a side, with bastions at each corner and walls pierced for cannon. It looked formidable. The Spaniards had cleared the forest for some distance around it to provide a field of fire for its guns.

"There's a lot wrong with that engineer's head," said Jed, after eyeing the angle of the fort and then the position of the gun platform. "He's putting the guns where they can't hit any side of the fort head on, only at an angle. See?" He pointed. "I wouldn't wager a ha'penny he knows what he's doing."

Sickness, which had disabled numbers of men ever since landing at Jamaica, now began to take a heavier toll. So many of the gunners of the army's small artillery corps had died or were ill that sailors had to be sent from ships to help man the growing number of guns now emplaced. When the guns on the platform began to beat at the walls of the fort the Spaniards replied, killing a few of the British gunners. What was even worse, the Spanish balls that overshot the gun platform battery fell directly into the camp that had been placed behind it. In an hour or so these stray shots killed or wounded over a hundred men.

To Greg's horrified regret, one of those killed was his own Captain Walker whom he had grown to like and respect even from a distance. It seemed ironic that he, the only native British captain of the four among the Virginia troops, should be one of the first of the colonial soldiers to fall. That part of the camp most exposed was hastily moved to safer ground.

Although the army ashore was having troubles, Admiral Vernon and Admiral Ogle were doing all they could to help by surprising and taking the fort and battery on the opposite side of the strait.

During the days of delay, Greg's company had been busily cutting fascines and stakes. Discontent with the way things were going was general both among the American contingent and among Lord Cavendish's regiment which was working in the woods at the same tasks. After talking with several of the regulars Jed returned, whistling in dismay.

"Don't sound good," he told Greg. "I knew ever since that day of the riot back in Jamaica that Wentworth was scared of his shadow. Now he's so timid he don't dare make a move."

On the following day they learned more when they ran into some Virginians from Captain Washington's company. Several of them were sitting in a circle, slapping mosquitoes and wishing they were home.

"It'll be a long time to that," said a sandy-haired man from the Northern Neck named Hall. "We get to hear what's going on and no one likes it," he explained to Greg and Jed.

"How do you hear?" asked Greg. He had been trying to figure out some way to get from Tierra Bomba to the mainland and do his errand and nothing had occurred to him.

"Our captain's on the Admiral's ship. Was made commander of the marines aboard it, so he has to stay there. Has an orderly named Ralph, and he comes ashore every chance he get to see his brother who's with us. Captain Washington likes the Admiral and the Admiral likes him. 'Course the Captain don't sit in on the councils they have most every day, but it's all talked over in front of him, like at dinner, and Ralph hears what they say. Wentworth won't attack the fort until the guns can make a big breach in the walls and we can march in all proper like. Vernon says he don't need a big breach, we can go up with scaling ladders and take it right away, says he's taking too much time and their guns are hurting us as bad as ours are hurting them."

They went on to agree that life on a ship wasn't fit for anything but a cockroach or a sailor, and it wasn't much better on land. The engineer officer was killed the next day by a cannon shot as he reconnoitered the fort. Many of the men felt that if it had only happened sooner a good deal of time and trouble would have been saved.

General Wentworth still delayed, declaring the fort had not yet been sufficiently damaged. As army commander, he could not be directly ordered by Vernon to attack the fort, or to do anything else. Both admirals were constantly urging him to take action, but when he refused they were helpless. At last more guns were in place and the whole battery fired alternating rounds of grapeshot and round shot continuously throughout a day and a night. In the morning it could be seen that the breach, already begun, had been greatly enlarged. Rumor spread that the attack would be that day.

Governor Gooch appeared in the American camp in the afternoon. "We are going for the fort in an hour or two," he said as the men gathered around him. "The grenadiers will lead. Following them will be five hundred men in small parties carrying scaling ladders and picks and axes in case they are needed. These will be supported by five hundred more men. That should be enough to do the trick. Now get your ladders and axes and form company ranks. Captain Mercer will be in immediate charge of the American detachment."

As the Governor turned to the pile of ladders the Jamaicans had prepared, Greg saw some British soldiers watching open-mouthed. Perhaps their Generals didn't talk to them man to man, he thought, and was glad he was a colonial.

At 5:30 in the afternoon the advance began, with a sergeant, twelve grenadiers and thirty volunteers in the vanguard. Then came the ranks of the imposing grenadiers. Three high curving mortar shells signaled the assault followed by a great blast of fire from the British guns on the platform, round shot aimed at the breach and grapeshot bursting among the Spanish infantrymen on the walls. These promptly vanished.

It seemed to Greg that every cannon in the fort was pointing straight at him. His mouth was dry. He glanced to right and left. The rows of faces were set, serious, watching the fort. A cannon ball ricocheted from a rocky ledge and spun screaming away.

As the grenadiers, in their high leather hats, began stolidly to mount the slope toward the fort, Governor Gooch pushed through the ranks of the Americans and took the lead, the gold braid on his red coat shining like a beacon. Three men to a ladder, picks and axes over their shoulders, the colonials followed him, matching the march of the grenadiers. Greg wished he had his musket, but none had been issued for the Americans. A cannon ball fell to the left of the company and the men closed slightly to the right.

Governor Gooch halted and turned around, planting his feet

firmly apart on the hillside, his back to the fort. "Don't cluster, men," he called. "Keep ranks and spread out."

At his last word a shower of dirt six feet high erupted in front of him. As it subsided all could see that a cannon ball had passed directly between the Governor's white-gaitered legs and buried itself in the ground before him. A look of incredulity spread over his face as he staggered. Captain Mercer sprang forward and caught him as he fell.

"No!" ordered Gooch loudly. "Not hurt. Help me stand. Go on, men."

Obediently, the Captain and one of his sergeants pulled him to his feet as his soldiers edged by him reluctantly. Blood was welling through the torn gaiters. "Missed me," he said stoutly, took a step forward and fell again.

Propping himself to a sitting position, he looked at his captain and the jostling soldiers. "Go ahead. I'll wait here." He raised his voice. "Go on, men. Don't linger. I'll be all right." He looked around at them and gestured with his head toward the fort. "Take up the ladders." He noticed Greg close by. "You. Wait. Get three others. I'll have to go back to the ship soon."

Captain Mercer ordered three men with a ladder to leave ranks and wait by the Governor. Then he again took up the advance, followed slowly by the men. One of the three beside Gooch took off his own shirt and tore it into strips and began to bind the Governor's bleeding legs.

The guns of the battery had stopped firing. "What's going on?" asked the Governor heavily.

"The grenadiers are near the fort and have halted, sir," Greg reported. "They're firing a volley at the men in the breach. Now they're going up over the stones. They're inside the fort." There came a few ragged shots and a cheer from behind the walls. "We've got it, sir."

"Good," replied Gooch. "Now take me back to a barge."

His face went white as they eased him onto the ladder; the blood made a dark trail on the dry ground as they carried him gently to the beach. As they waited there Greg could see that the iron chain and boom across the channel was no longer in place to hold back the British ships. A series of explosions and a welling cloud of smoke showed at least one of the Spanish warships had blown up.

The four Virginians saw their Governor lifted into a long boat by sailors and then trotted back through the camp to where the attack had begun, intending to go on to the fort. But they found the Americans returning with their ladders and gear. The garrison of the fort had retreated out of the far gate and vanished into the woods. By evening all the blockading Spanish ships were sunk. Apparently all was over for the time being.

Although the British men-of-war and transports could now sail through the passage and into the wide lagoon beyond, more time passed before the troops and their stores could re-embark. Strong winds raised such a high surf that the boats from the ships could not come close to shore. But at length tents were struck, cannon dragged down and heaved into barges, the sick carried to the hospital ships, and Greg and Jed once more found themselves on board the *Hampton Court*.

"More room now," Jed observed as they filed below decks. "That's what the fever does. We can spread out a bit."

How many more men would they lose, Greg wondered. If only there had not been so many delays! He had not been on the ship an hour before a sergeant came looking for him. "The General wants you and your friend in his cabin," he announced, "and now."

The Governor was sitting up in his bed, his bandaged legs stretched out before him. He nodded to their salute. "We need help here. My man's done his best, but he's about worn out. Would you be willing to help change dressings, bring up the food, and," smiling at Greg, "read to me?"

"Yes, sir," they said together. "Gladly." "It'll go better with three," Jed added.

Greg was shocked at the sight of the Governor's legs between the ankles and the knees for they were black with bruises and oozing blood. The only treatment advised by the ship's barber-surgeon had been to wash them often with salt water; the rest was up to time and nature. It was lucky that no bones had been broken. The Governor insisted that afternoon on trying to walk so he could get on deck, but it took the three to carry him there, and settle him in a chair. While standing in the sun and wind they saw a sloop suddenly break out its sails and turn to the north.

"That's the *Spence*," the Governor told them, "taking dispatches to England to tell of the capture of Boca Chica. I hear General Wentworth, and even Admiral Ogle, didn't want to send them, thinking the announcement too early because the people will take it as assured that we have Cartagena in our grasp. Wentworth may be right, this time, but Admiral Vernon insisted."

Greg's heart gave a lurch as he realized the sloop would stop at Kingston and Mr. Woodford also would believe that Cartagena would soon fall and send out his own schooner to meet Mr. Ogden. There was not much time left for him to find the merchant.

S E V E N

Greg Takes a Chance

PONDEROUSLY the towering men-of-war crept through the narrows, skirting the floating markers which had been placed above the hulls of sunken Spanish ships, and dropped anchors in the lake-like harbor. With the fleet again assembled, on the next day, the movement toward the inner harbor of Cartagena began.

Not long after the *Hampton Court* got under way Greg was summoned from below to report to Governor Gooch, who had been carried to the high poop deck at the stern. He found the Governor, his feet propped on a stool, morosely eyeing the slowly passing shoreline. Returning Greg's salute, the Governor motioned to another stool. "Sit down, lad. I want you to read to me. Here is the book."

For a time Governor Gooch seemed to listen but gradually he grew restive and at last told Greg to stop. "It is difficult to keep my mind on what you read," he explained.

"Sir," ventured Greg, wanting to show his sympathy but hesitating at the gulf between them, "it is grievous to see you downcast. But it should not be long now until we take this city; then you can go back to Jamaica and recover properly."

"Aye. But while I sit here and do nothing I cannot be cheerful." The Governor's tone was almost savage. "I am a helpless hulk. With Wentworth in command of the army, I have a feeling we may not capture the place at all."

Greg was surprised, for it was not Governor Gooch's habit to speak so frankly about the commanding general. He must be in low spirits indeed, but he sounded resigned instead of angry as he went on. "I am thinking that when we get further up the harbor there may be a chance for shore parties to forage. Fruits, vegetables, chicken, or pork would be welcomed by the company and the ship's crew. If I can, I will ask the Captain to put some of our people ashore."

Greg kept his face impassive. Ever since the victory at Boca Chica he had been wondering how he could possibly manage to get to the *Casa Hermosa*. "I'd be glad to join the party, sir," he said calmly. "And as soon as possible."

In the mid-afternoon the ships of the line rounded the second of the most easterly points of the jutting peninsula of Tierra Bomba, the one Mr. Woodford had shown on the map as pointing in the general direction of the hill on the shore where stood Ogden's house. Some two miles ahead was the inner harbor, a rounded basin a mile and a half in diameter. It lay behind two slender points of land with a channel a little more than half a mile wide between them. On the tip of one peninsula stood a strong fort named Castillo Grande, on the opposite point a fascine battery called Manzanillo. The channel was said to be shallow in places, but the English had trustworthy charts and could avoid shoals.

Depths of water were known, but what the English did not know was the exact strength of the fort and the battery, whether the Spaniards would defend them vigorously, and what obstructions might have been placed in the channel. It was suspected that some ships had been sunk in it because of distant explosions heard from their anchorage at Boca Chica. As they cautiously approached the entrance a sudden bloom of flame and smoke showed the Spaniards had blown up a ship in the inner harbor. It was later found to have been a French merchantman, destroyed to keep it from falling into English hands. This was taken as a good sign; the Spaniards would not defend the inner harbor but would wait for the British to land. When the British ships threw a few shells at the fort and battery there was no reply. Both had been abandoned. It was now near sunset and the fleet anchored outside the harbor.

At dawn boats were launched to take soundings, and it was soon found that vessels had indeed been sunk to block the channel. The navy was set the task of removing them, which might take a day or so. On hearing this, the Governor brought out his plan to land foragers. Greg and Jed, congratulating themselves on their luck, were in the first boat. Because of the heat all the soldiers left their coats and hats on the ship and tied bandanas around their heads as protection against the sun.

The only place they could expect to find food of any kind was the eastern shore of the lagoon, some two miles away. As they neared the mainland they saw they were approaching a mangrove swamp, so the boats were turned to where there was a clear reach of shore near the mouth of a creek.

As the boats grounded the lieutenant leaped out, picked a half dozen sailors to stay with the craft and ordered the rest of the men to divide into four small parties to scour the surrounding area. "There is a road around this side of the lagoon," he said. "And there is supposed to be a small village somewhere. If you meet unarmed people of the countryside don't harm them. You are to fire only if you run into armed opposition. We'll meet here in four hour's time. I will lead one party, the bos'n another; the other two are to act independently."

Jed and Greg joined the last of the parties. They soon came on to the narrow road and followed it south, gradually falling behind the others. They knew the hill and the house were near the road but would be hard to see because of the trees and bushes. When the men ahead were out of sight around a bend Jed pulled Greg through a space in the brush. "Let's get off the road. I want to look around."

They pushed through the thinning underbrush until Jed found a tall tree with spreading branches. "Give me a boost," he told Greg, who wished he had thought of the idea himself. He pushed Jed up until he could grasp the lowest branch and pull himself up the trunk. In a few minutes he was down.

"We're all right," he reported. "There're two hills opposite, but back from the road. There's another ahead and closer to the track. A road leads up from this one to a gray stone house atop that nearer hill. There's a small village a piece ahead and some of our men are near it. And there's something that looks like a cloud of dust a mile or more beyond. Can't make out what it is. Let's go on to this *Hermosa*."

Greg grinned at him. "Couldn't get along without you, Jed. And if these people don't speak English you'll understand them somehow, anyway."

Jed smiled in embarrassed pleasure. "Ever since I got myself into this mess I've been glad you're along. Makes it more interesting."

They kept going until they came to the road up the hill and climbed that until they reached two gateposts, one carved *Casa* and the other *Hermosa*. Here a driveway wound in sweeping curves between rows of palms to a long, low pleasant house set amid flowering shrubs on a terrace. The view of the harbor was magnificent, and Greg wished he had time to enjoy and examine it. Instead, he marched to the door and pulled a hanging chain beside it. A gong sounded, a tiny window in the door opened, and two eyes peered at them.

"Mr. Ogden," said Greg loudly. "We want to see Mr. Ogden."

The eyes vanished, but through the opening they heard a woman call a question in Spanish.

"Soldados," came the guttural reply. "Extranjeros."

"Inglés?"

"Si, Señorita," was the slow reluctant answer.

The woman said something sharply in Spanish and grudgingly the door swung open. A short, swarthy man holding a musket stood at one side, glaring. Facing them was a middle-aged woman, with graying hair and hazel eyes in a high-necked white dress, who could only be English.

Greg and Jed bowed. "Mrs Ogden?" inquired Greg hopefully.

"Gracious, no." Her laugh was friendly and a little excited. "I am Miss Gaynor, the governess."

"Then is Mr. Ogden at home? I need to see him on—on business, quickly, if you please."

"I assure you it would please me if you could." She paused, "You aren't English soldiers," she accused, staring at their uniforms.

"We are with the British army, but we are Americans, Virginians."

"Really? How interesting! You are the first Americans I have ever seen. I should like to know your country. You *must* see Mr. Ogden?"

"Yes. Please. It's on business—from Jamaica."

"Since it is business of course you should. But I am sorry to have to tell you, young man, that Mr. Ogden and his wife went in to their town house in Cartagena when our ships first appeared off the city. Because of your landing parties, he felt he would be cut off from his business affairs if he stayed here. I think he rather doubts that you will take the city. The Spaniards have been building up their defenses, oh, for over two months, ever since they learned the attack was coming."

"But, then, why are you—?" Greg began.

"I am here with the children because it was felt safer for them. Also, with the rainy season starting any day now, it will be more healthy on higher ground."

Greg's shoulders sagged in bitter disappointment. "I promised—," he said dully.

"If our army should capture the city you will find him at his home on a street leading north from the central plaza and two blocks east of the cathedral. You can recognize the house for it is at the corner of the second block and it has distinctive double doors studded with square brass nails and has also a small watch tower on the roof. He will be there until the fighting is over."

"And then we'll be gone," put in Jed flatly.

"I am sorry you have had a fruitless journey. How did you get ashore? We watched the fleet yesterday. It makes one proud to be English when one sees our ships and flags."

"We came ashore, ma'am, looking for fresh food for our Governor, who was wounded at Boca Chica, and for others on the ship."

"We can furnish you some fresh food, at least." She turned to the still glowering man and issued rapid orders in Spanish. He shouldered his musket and slouched down the hall. "José will bring you some eggs, chickens, fruits, vegetables. That is all we can gather quickly."

She opened the door and stepped on to the terrace. "We could see the smoke, you know, and hear the firing, so we knew there was fighting. I wished every day I could know what was happening."

"They're clearing the passage to the inner harbor now," volunteered Jed. "We took all the forts they didn't run away from."

Greg scarcely listened. By now the sloop *Spence* would be nearing Jamaica with the Admiral's news. Soon Mr. Woodford would send his own schooner to the bay beyond the Paso Caballos. And Mr. Ogden would not have had the message in time. Perhaps after the city fell? No, that might take days, the way Wentworth would conduct a siege, and every day the schooner remained in the bay would increase its danger.

Miss Gaynor was still admiring the ships when there came the sound of a spatter of shots in the direction of the village to the south. As they turned to look they saw, now much nearer, the dust cloud Jed had noticed when up in the tree.

"Our foragers have run into whatever is raising that dust," muttered Jed.

"It must be the cattle drive," exclaimed Miss Gaynor. "José said yesterday that some of the farmers and herdsmen from further along the shore were going to drive cattle into Cartagena in the hope of good prices before the siege really begins."

The foragers have met them, thought Greg. His next thought was that some of the herdsmen were armed and had tried to defend their property. They would be angry with the soldiers. But the dust cloud was rolling along rapidly on the road below the hill. Apparently most of the herdsmen and their cattle had escaped from the clash. Suddenly, a daring idea flashed into his mind.

He turned impetuously to the governess. "Miss Gaynor. I need clothes such as those herders are wearing. What are they? Can you get any for me?"

Miss Gaynor nearly lost her British composure. "What on earth for?" she exclaimed.

Jed's eyes narrowed as he studied Greg speculatively.

"Don't you see? It's a chance to get into Cartagena. My only chance. I'll pass myself off as a herdsman driving cattle."

"You're crazy," said Jed sharply.

"Look, Jed," appealed Greg. "You know I've got to get to Mr. Ogden. If I wait until we take the place it will be too late. We owe Mr. Woodford too much to let him down."

Jed shook his head. "You don't know Spanish."

"I'll play deaf and dumb."

"How're you going to get out?"

"Same way I get in. I'll take that chance. Please, Miss Gaynor, can you help me?"

The governess hesitated, glancing at Jed. "It's dangerous," she murmured, "but ingenious."

"What are you going to do with your pants and gaiters?" Jed asked sourly.

"Leave them here. I can come back later."

"Well—." It was Jed's turn to hesitate.

Admiration shone in Miss Gaynor's eyes. "You may be a colonial," she said, "but you are truly British. Since you are determined, I will get the things for you. I am the daughter of a British officer, you see." She glanced at them almost gaily, swung on her heels and disappeared down the hall.

"She's a nice lady, don't waste words," said Jed admiringly. "But what'll I tell the Governor?"

"Tell him I went on a special mission for Mr. Woodford. He, too, owes a good deal to Mr. Woodford's help. Tell him I'll be back as soon as possible."

In a moment Miss Gaynor returned with a well-worn tan shirt, a pair of loose white trousers that ended just below the knees, a pair of sandals, a straw hat to replace the bandana, and a long knife, such as used by the natives to clear the brush, attached to a belt of rope. "These should about fit you, lad. You can change in the first room to the right of the hall. I will see your uniform safely hidden."

Greg quickly slipped into his disguise and emerged for inspection. Miss Gaynor looked him over. "That will do quite well, I think, especially since you are so well tanned." Her smile and her lively voice showed she was enjoying the conspiracy.

"I'd better come along with you," Jed muttered.

"You can't. Though I'd like to have you. You'll have to carry the baskets of food to the Governor. He'd be furious if we both disappeared; he might even send out a detail to look for us."

As Greg shook hands and tried to thank Miss Gaynor her eyes suddenly filled with tears. "God bless you," she murmured. "I will pray for your safe return to your ship."

Halfway down the hill Jed set down his two baskets and grasped Greg's hand. "Cut yourself a stout stick with that knife—that's what they drive the beasts with. Be careful. Don't take chances unless you have to. If anyone gets suspicious drop out into the woods and get away fast. I'm heading for the boats now. The others'll be too busy slaughtering and skinning the cattle they've taken to pay much mind to me." He picked up the baskets and angled off down the hill. "Good luck," he called back over his shoulder, as though he had almost forgotten to say it. Greg saw him disappear into some bushes, obviously to wait until the cattle and herders had passed.

Heading for a spot where he hoped he would intercept the cattle, Greg hurried to the road and waited behind some bushes of his own until most of the anxious, swarthy men had passed. They were angry and frightened, chattering at each other vehemently. A few of them carried muskets, but most were armed only with the long knives such as Miss Gaynor had given him and sticks for prodding the cattle. It was evident that the British foragers had not met a very stubborn defense.

A stray steer wandered from the herd and stopped to munch some dust-covered grass. Greg boldly stepped from behind his shelter and with his stick began to beat and prod the scrawny animal into motion.

They came to a creek and watered the animals at the ford, and then had trouble getting the herd to move again. In the process one man shouted at Greg, who tried to look stupid and made signs he hoped indicated he could not speak because he was dumb. The fellow stared at him, shrugged, and went about his business.

It seemed to Greg that hours passed while the herd made its slow-paced way along the road which now was running through more open country where tall trees were thinly spaced. The day had begun in bright, hot sunshine, but the sky had become overcast, for which Greg, breathing the dust kicked up by the herd and sweating profusely, was thankful. The road ran in curving scallops, now along the shore, now back between groves of trees or sun-browned fields until, rounding one of the curves, a man ahead shouted "La Popa." He was pointing to a conical wooded hill that rose abruptly from the plain, holding on its summit a building with a gold cross on the top. Greg recognized it as the taller hill he had seen when the fleet passed Cartagena. They were getting close to the city.

As they entered a narrow defile between the foot of the hill and a small lagoon of the bay, he heard the thud of guns from the direction of the inner harbor. Small as it might be, some British ships had made their way through passage of the last harbor! The shots would be from bomb ketches of shallow draft that had been moved in to bombard the city itself. A sudden fear came to Greg. Would he be too late? It would be terrible to be penned inside the city while it was attacked by his own army. Somewhat the same thought occurred to the herdsmen, for they redoubled their shouts and beat the cattle more enthusiastically.

There came another cry, "San Lazaro," and Greg gazed up at the fort that guarded the landward side of Cartagena, the fort the British must take before they could capture the city. San Lazaro stood on a hill, lower than that of La Popa, and less than a quarter mile distant. Its slope, about sixty feet high, he guessed, seemed just as steep. He could glimpse the snouts of two guns on the wall facing the road and two more at corner bastions. Below the walls was a line of newly dug earth. Climbing that hill with pack and musket would be a breath-taking, muscle-straining task for any soldier.

They left the hill and its fort on their right and came to a short peninsula between an arm of the harbor and a small bay. A causeway led from the end of the peninsula to the gray walls of what at first seemed to be another fort, but when they reached a gate Greg saw the place was a small walled town, crowded with houses facing narrow streets, and realized it was the island suburb marked "Hihimani" on Mr. Woodford's map. The herd clattered along a street where people scattered into open doorways to escape the horns and hooves, then through another gate to another short causeway that led to the main gate of the city. With some difficulty, the herd was goaded and beaten toward the entrance where soldiers grinned and shouted jests at the struggling drivers. Thus Greg passed between the massive walls, beneath a fortified gate, and, poking at a head-tossing steer, entered the enemy city of Cartagena.

Beyond the gate was an open square where soldiers could parade and guard could be changed. This turned into a wide street lined

with solid-looking two-story stone houses with iron-barred doors and windows, red-tiled roofs and balconies of carved wood or wrought ironwork. It was a handsome place, with an air of stability and wealth. Most of the British shells thrown at the city must have fallen short or hit the fortifications, for there appeared to be little damage, so far, to the houses. After passing two streets that crossed at right angles the cattle drivers came to an open square or plaza with a grassy park in its center and a row of palm trees around the edges. Facing this square, at its far corner, was a magnificent church. The twin towers rose, from a carved and decorated façade, far above the surrounding roofs.

"La Catedral," murmured the herdsman beyond and made the sign of the cross.

The cattle were halted around the plaza but began to mill about, attempting to escape down the streets or to get into the park to eat the grass, while the men ran around waving their sticks. A column of soldiers entered the square to help separate the herd into groups to be driven away, while people began to gather to watch, at a safe distance, or to bargain for the meat to come. A shell burst a few blocks away. The gunners were getting the range.

This would be a good time to leave, Greg thought. He remembered Miss Gaynor's directions. The street he wanted took off from the square of the cathedral, quite close at hand, just to his right. He watched for an opportunity to slip away, though he was sure no one was noticing him.

The moment came almost at once. With a tremendous crash a big British mortar bomb hit the roof of the cathedral. Fragments of wooden beams flew higher than the towers. There was a second, greater explosion and flames shot from the shattered windows. Greg wondered what had made that second explosion. At once all was confusion. The cattle bellowed and stampeded. Women shrieked and fell on their knees. Soldiers and herdsmen shouted. A bell, two, three, then more, began to peal out frantically over the city. Men carrying pails of sand came rushing from all the streets. Greg slipped quickly away. They will be kept busy for quite a while, he thought, as he walked along looking for the house with the brass-studded doors and a watch tower on the roof.

EIGHT

Within the Walls of Cartagena

THE street was grim and forbidding. The walls of the houses seemed to press in on the narrow way, giving an air of closeness and secrecy, and the heavy iron bars at the infrequent windows enhanced the air of concealment. The scattered reflections of the glow from the cathedral fire were ominous. Behind Greg the monotonous boom of the English guns, mingled with shouts from the crowd and the crackle of flames, added to his sense of urgency. For a moment he feared that his directions had been wrong, but then the brass decorations of a door shone in the momentary glow from the mounting fire and he saw the watchtower on top of the house. The feeling of triumph with which he pulled the bell chain made him forget his weariness and thirst and hunger.

The tiny window in the door slid open. "Mr. Ogden," said Greg. "Mr. Ogden. I must see him."

The window closed, but before Greg could protest there was a clanking sound from within and one door swung ajar.

"Mr. Ogden," he said again. "From Mr. Woodford."

A hand pulled him inside. He could see he was in a driveway, a kind of tunnel beneath the second floor of the house, wide enough for a coach and pair. At the end was a round, brick-walled garden nearly filled with flowering plants and bushes. A fountain tinkled gently in the center. The figure beside him asked, "Who are you?" The accent was English. "Quite evidently you are not what you appear to be—a peasant."

"I'm an American," replied Greg. "From the English fleet. I came ashore to find Mr. Ogden. I have a message for him from Mr. Woodford of Jamaica. It's important."

"Ah, I see." There was a pause. "Mr. Ogden is occupied at the moment. But come with me." The tone was kindly. "No doubt you are hungry and thirsty after your—er—exertions."

The man led the way to the enclosed garden. A vine covered with star shaped flowers climbed to an open balcony that encircled the second floor. After the heat and dust of the road the garden, with its sound of water falling gently, was restful and refreshing. The guide turned to an open corridor to the right, past a window through which came voices.

"Both of us know that when a city is taken there is profit for more than the conquerors," said a low, rasping voice.

"What do you seek this time?" asked another man.

"Emeralds, first of all. Then gold, pearls, whatever transports easily, before the English get them, if they take the city. But it's emeralds I'm after." The voices faded to a mumble.

The man beside Greg pointed to a bench along the wall of the house and well out of earshot of the room they had passed. "Wait here," he directed. "You will be attended to promptly."

In a few moments a servant girl came out of a far door bringing a basin of water and a towel which she placed on the bench beside Greg. As he washed, gratefully, the sound of the harsh voice persisted in his ears. It was familiar. He had heard it before, but he could not remember where. The girl reappeared with a plate of cold meat and bread and, when Greg pointed to the fountain, a goblet of water.

While he ate, Greg kept trying to place the voice. Should he take a chance and creep back to the open window to hear more? It would be risky, for he could be seen from the windows around the garden. The decision was taken from him when a door was flung open and a man in a dark suit emerged. He halted to call back, "It's a deal, then."

That turn of the head gave Greg a clear view of the man's face. He was Walter Quinzaine, and Greg realized that the last time he had heard the rasping voice had been in the bare office of Quinzaine's house in Kingston. What was he doing here, and speaking of emeralds?

Quinzaine noticed Greg, glanced at him curiously, and was about to leave when he stared again. He approached slowly, his eyes narrowed in concentration as he peered at Greg in the fading light. Greg wished he had not taken off his hat. Quinzaine halted and spoke questioningly in Spanish. Greg pointed to his mouth, shook his head and made vague signs.

Quinzaine watched him intently. "You are English, aren't you?" he snapped.

Greg repeated his signs.

"Yes. I know you now. You were brought to my house with a message for Woodford. Well. Well."

He stood still a long minute. At last, without another word, he turned, paused at the open door as if to re-enter it, then strode by it quickly and on to the carriage-way that led to the street.

Scarcely had the privateer disappeared when Greg's guide beckoned to him. The room they entered served as both office and library for it held a bookshelf and several chairs as well as desks. A man rose behind the larger of the desks. He was of medium height and compactly built, with broad shoulders and long arms. The guide lighted a lamp, whispered a word, and vanished. Now, as the man gestured for Greg to sit down, he could see more clearly the ruddy face, strong features, and brown eyes, which, Greg felt, surveyed the world with a mingling of amusement and craft, and belonged to a man who could hold his own in any circumstance.

"I am Ogden," he announced genially. "I am told you say you have a message from Woodford of Jamaica. That means you must be from the fleet. How did you get ashore and into that rig?"

Greg explained he had been with foragers but had borrowed the clothes and joined the cattle drive into the city.

Mr. Ogden chuckled. "Resourceful of you. Yes, when I was in the patio I heard the arrival of the cattle and the explosion of the powder they thought was safely stored in the cathedral. They'll not have that fire out too soon." He paused, then asked in a harder tone, "How did you know where to find me?"

"Mr. Woodford told me how to find your country place." Greg tried to make his voice as stiff as the other's. "Miss Gaynor told me how I could recognize your house."

"How can I know you come from Mr. Woodford? You do not have the right accent."

"I am from Virginia."

"One of our livelier colonies, though unfortunately not so wealthy in trade as some others. But we must look to the future, so we have our associates there, such as Captain Bartlett and Mr. Jason Pollock. It must have been Pollock who sent you to Woodford in the first place. Well, produce your credentials."

"I was to show you this." Greg tugged off the signet ring and held it out across the desk. The other took it delicately, held it close to the lamp turning it this way and that and tapping the stone with a small dagger. "Yes." Suddenly he was genial again. "This is the ring he uses as a seal. I cannot doubt you." He laid the ring on the desk. Greg reached for it quickly and slipped it back on his finger. That was to be returned to Mr. Woodford.

"Now, what is the message?" inquired Mr. Ogden.

Greg repeated it slowly and carefully. At the mention of emeralds he fancied Mr. Ogden's eyes flickered, though that might have been his own imagination. At the end Mr. Ogden rubbed his chin thoughtfully. "It could be arranged," he murmured. "There are always emeralds in Cartagena. Nueva Granada is the greatest producer of those stones in the world and most of them go out through the city."

Still rubbing his chin, he went on, "The sloop *Spence* should be at Kingston by now with tidings of the fall of Boca Chica—which will be enlarged upon and no doubt taken as news of the fall of the city itself. Seven more days for the Woodford vessel to reach the Bay of Barbacoas."

"Then you can get the emeralds?" That was the one thing Greg had to know, that would make all this effort worth while.

"Of course. I will bring them myself to the rendezvous. It may call for fat bribes in certain hands to round up that many stones of good quality in the short time. But never fear. I have much influence in this place, let me tell you. Woodford's ship can and should wait four or five days at the bay. I will have this collection gathered within ten or twelve days, siege or no siege. Wealthy planters have been sending their gold and jewels into the city for safe-keeping from marauders of all kinds. Take my word for it, lad, I will take care of the order to Mr. Woodford's complete satisfaction." And he beamed at Greg.

"Yes, sir. I truly hope so. Now I must get back to my ship. Have you any suggestions as to how?"

"I think you must trust to your own ingenuity. You were clever enough about getting in."

Greg hesitated. It was on the tip of his tongue to tell the merchant that he had recognized his visitor and that Quinzaine had recognized him and might be a danger. But caution stopped him. There was something a bit odd about all this. And what did he know about Ogden anyway? He looked out of the window. The quick tropical twilight had become night. "Might I stay here until morning?" he asked, more timidly than he had intended.

"Certainly not," was the quick reply. "There will be quite a to-do about the cathedral fire. If by chance your disguise were penetrated it would be hard to explain why I was sheltering one of King George's colonial soldiers."

"But, sir, just now you were—er—claiming—I mean you indicated that you had much influence here. If this is so, could you not by some means help me to leave the city?"

Mr. Ogden's eyes widened, then he guffawed, slapped his thigh and sat down in his chair, overcome with laughter. "B'gad, you really are clever, lad. You have me on the hip." Still chuckling he took a sheet of crested paper from a drawer, dipped a quill in the inkpot in front of him and rapidly scrawled a short message. He next opened a drawer of the desk, took out a page of writing, and

carefully copied a signature below the lines he had penned. He waved the paper to dry it and handed it to Greg.

"There. You have a very good pass, signed by the highest authority in Cartagena." He chuckled again. "All you have to do is show it to the sentry at the gate. I do this not for King George, God save him, but because you have given me amusement. Once you are safely away from the city I charge you to destroy this—and I really believe you will."

Greg stammered his thanks. This man was a strange person, not one to be understood easily. "I trust, sir, you will find Mr. Woodford's schooner without difficulty."

"That I shall, my lad, that I shall," replied Mr. Ogden.

The guide was waiting with a lantern to show him through the passageway to the street, now a place of darkness and black shadows. Slowly he made his way back to the plaza where the people of Cartagena were still bringing baskets of dirt and sand to throw on the smoldering fire inside the walls of the cathedral. The red light, flaring and dying, through the windows cast an eerie light across the plaza and the silent, hurrying throngs. Gladly he retraced his steps to the city gate. When the sentries on guard stopped him, he showed the message and waited, heart in throat. The three soldiers examined the signature, gave him a look of surprised respect, and motioned him through.

He followed the narrow streets of the small island suburb to the second gate, was waved through and, in case anyone was watching, slowly crossed the causeway to the mainland. As soon as he found a substantial tree trunk he sat down with his back against it and let out a deep, grateful sigh. He was free.

Though tree trunk and ground were hard, Greg was so comfortable sitting instead of walking that he was about to doze off when the sound of marching men and the rattle of accoutrements roused him. He hid behind the tree. A long file of Spanish soldiers was passing on the trail. Reinforcements for San Lazaro, he thought, and remembered he must get past the men working there and on through the defile at the foot of the taller hill beyond while darkness made that possible. He waited a bit after the last soldier had passed, then followed cautiously, hoping to hear, through the buzz and humming of night insects, any sound of danger. He did not dare even to slap at the mosquitoes that seemed determined to eat him alive.

When he neared the place on the road where it passed between the foot of the hill of San Lazaro and the nearby shore he stopped and looked up at the fort. By the light of torches the Spaniards were still working furiously, digging a trench and throwing up earthworks on the side of the steep hill below the sheer walls. Each hour they were making it harder for the English to carry the place by assault. After studying what was being done as well as he could in the darkness, he took to the woods near the shore, working his way toward the defile between hill and lagoon.

He had not gone far when there was an earsplitting crash near at hand, followed by the thud of a cannon from an English ship. Another explosion followed, and another. The ship was trying to bombard the workers on San Lazaro, but the shots were falling short, in fact, he realized with dismay, they were falling around him. He had better get out of the place fast. He made his way back to the road and along it to the foot of the higher hill, seeking shelter. It seemed a long time before he reached a rocky outcrop of the hill and found, by feeling with his hands, a place which put the rock between him and the falling shot. Here he settled, feeling fairly secure. The British ship seemed to be scattering its fire over the general area, the gunners apparently imagining Spanish soldiers were there in great numbers. At last the shelling slowed, then stopped. Greg went to sleep.

He awoke shivering in the coolness of the tropical dawn. He was hungry and thirsty, but there was little to be done about that. As he stretched the kinks out of arms and legs he considered his course. Likely the best thing would be to return to the *Casa Hermosa* where Miss Gaynor would give him something to eat and he could recover his uniform. After that he would hope to rejoin the regiment when the British came ashore. He returned to the road and came into the open country beyond the defile.

After a half hour of brisk walking, with no sign of a Spaniard, he glanced toward the lagoon and saw two boats filled with men approaching the shore. He crawled under a low-drooping bush to watch. The boats were beached a hundred yards away. As the crews scrambled out Greg joyfully recognized the red jackets and green lapels of the American regiment. The men formed ranks and, leaving the British sailors by the boats, headed for the road. Greg restrained his impulse to dash out and meet them; they were armed and might shoot first and ask questions later.

When they neared his bush he called out, "Hello, there. I'm Gregory Shelby of Virginia. I'm coming out. Hold your fire."

Instantly the group halted and looked in his direction. He recognized Jed—and Sam. This was good luck beyond imagining! He pushed aside the branches and strode toward them.

"By all that's holy," roared Jed. "Did you make it, Greg?"

"Yes."

"Where in blazes have you been?" demanded Sergeant Simmons, staring at Greg's clothes.

"Cartagena," answered Greg simply.

"Don't believe it."

"Greg, I'm pure joyed to see you," said Sam, beaming as the others crowded around and fired questions. He told them he had had a message to deliver from the merchant who had befriended the troops in Kingston to a merchant in the city and then had been given a pass through the gates. "Then I got shelled and had to hide out the night."

"The *Weymouth*," said Simmons. "It got moved in close yesterday to shell the shore. At a council meeting yesterday the Admiral forced the scared cat to start things, so Wentworth and his grenadiers are landing pretty soon."

The Americans had something to do before that happened. The beef brought back by the foragers on the previous day had whetted the appetite of Governor Gooch, Sir Digby Dent, the ship's captain, and the appetites of the captains of several other vessels for more. The group had been sent ashore to take any other cattle being driven to Cartagena. Wentworth didn't know about it and wouldn't approve if he did.

"He'll be mad as a hornet if he finds us here," said Jed cheerfully.

Greg suggested that La Popa hill might be a good place to serve as a lookout for cattle because they could be seen at a distance and in time to get down and ambush them in the defile.

"Good idea," approved the Sergeant. "But what's up there?"

Greg admitted he didn't know.

"Might as well find out," said someone. "Kind of like to see a Spanish soldier, now I've come this far," agreed another. It was good to be on land again and carefree. Simmons grinned and started down the road.

It was more than a mile to the foot of the hill, which rose gently at first but soon became quite steep. Scrambling up, the Americans soon reached the summit and the monastery and chapel which could be seen from the sea and the harbor. They halted at the edge of the flat cleared space around the buildings.

"Steady," cautioned the Sergeant. "If there are any Spaniards we better rush the place and surprise them." The men went into a half crouch. Greg wished he had a musket. "Now," said Simmons.

They dashed across to the door of the monastery. It opened without hindrance on a group of amazed Spanish soldiers who were finishing their breakfast. Without even trying to grab their muskets they began piling out of a side door and down the hill. A half dozen, trapped, meekly surrendered.

"Good job," approved the Sergeant, smiling widely. Putting two men on guard over the prisoners, he ordered the rest to collect the abandoned weapons. With a musket in his hand Greg felt better. As they left the building they stopped and gazed down on Fort San Lazaro and its toilers.

Staring at it, Greg realized that La Popa commanded the lower fort. "All we have to do is put a battery up here and blow them out of those ditches," he said to Sergeant Simmons.

"So we could," agreed the Sergeant. "I hope Wentworth's men get here in time to do it before the Spaniards have sense enough to retake this hill."

"Hope them cattle get here first," said a man. "Don't see nothing coming on the road."

They all turned to peer anxiously along the narrow track. A man shouted "Boats! Coming into that shore over there. Anything that comes along on the road they'll get first."

Through the gathering haze over the harbor, tiny in the distance, could be seen 20 or 30 boats packed with troops.

"Kicked into action," muttered Jed. "That's the *Weymouth* back of them with the bare poles, couldn't get closer on account of shoals. That's why they're landing so far away."

The Americans on La Popa watched as the boats reached shore, discharged the troops, and returned to the ships. Even now Wentworth was taking his time for there was a delay until a small column of English began a cautious advance across the open country.

Jed snorted in disgust. "Afraid of an ambush in the open! Can't see any cannon with 'em. They'll get here by noon, if then."

Greg swung around to look again at the fort below. The slope of the hill of San Lazaro was steep, but not impossible to climb, and from what he could glimpse the side toward Cartagena appeared more gentle. The fort itself was a thick square of stone walls, 15 to 20 feet high, with six cannon on each of the four sides. A wide new trench was being dug, with the earth thrown up as a rampart at the top of the slope of grass and rocks.

Once more Jed was right, for the sun stood directly overhead when the column of grenadiers reached the foot of La Popa and began to climb. They were led by a Colonel Grant, who had a reputation for bravery and ability, and were accompanied by General Wentworth and an engineer officer. As the puffing, sweating General reached the crest, his unbelieving eyes saw Sergeant Simmons and his men standing stiffly at smart salute.

"What—what—who are you?" bellowed Wentworth when he got back his breath.

"American foragers, sir," replied the Sergeant. "General Gooch sent us to cut off cattle being driven into the city. We thought this a good place to watch out for them."

"Cattle! Foragers!" spluttered the General, his face mottled red with anger. "Colonials again! Undisciplined colonials!"

Greg was angry at the words, but at the same time felt a sort of sympathy for this martinet of a general who did not know what to do in emergencies and who was so outraged at despised colonials beating him to the capture of La Popa. The Sergeant was discreetly silent.

"I presume you have boats," sneered the General after an obvious struggle for control. "Get back to them at once. And to your ships."

The Sergeant saluted again. "Yes, sir," he said. "But, General, with all respect, we think if cannon could be mounted here they would command Fort San Lazaro down there."

"Sergeant," said Wentworth icily, "I do not need advice from colonials on how to conduct a siege."

When they reached the ship they reported despondently to the Captain and next to the Governor in his cabin. Sergeant Simmons told his story: no cattle, and the General was furious with them for taking La Popa.

"It's too bad, Sergeant," said Gooch sadly. "Wentworth has probably missed his best chance of taking Cartagena at once. He should have marched in today as fast as his men could go, as de Pointis did." He muttered something to himself about having to suffer fools. "My thanks, men," he said to those in the cabin. "You did your best, and it was not your fault the cattle didn't come and the General did." His eyes fell on Greg. "What is the meaning of that ridiculous costume?" he demanded sharply.

"It was necessary to accomplish a mission for Mr. Woodford, sir."

"By the Lord Harry! If it was anybody but Woodford I'd have you lashed. No more of such foolhardy nonsense. Sergeant, tell the Quartermaster to issue a new uniform to Shelby." With an ill-concealed twinkle in his eyes he added to Greg. "When you are properly clothed you will report back to me to give an account of your actions."

This Greg did later, though he made no mention of emeralds.

NINE

San Lazaro

ONCE Sergeant Simmons had said that most of a war was just waiting, and it was certainly true at Cartagena, Greg thought. The irritation of the troops turned to anger and their anger to near despair as Wentworth, fearing ambushes wherever he moved, doggedly landed more men, cannon, and supplies. He called on the fleet to bombard San Lazaro—which it couldn't reach effectively without risk of grounding ships in shallow lagoons—and obviously was working by the strict rules of formal siege warfare. In turn, the impatient Admiral demanded that troops storm the high strong walls of the fort and carry them immediately. Unless Wentworth could be forced to an assault, the army would be there another month. Meanwhile, British soldiers and sailors and Americans were dying from yellow fever.

On the day after the landing all of the remaining American captains came to call on their general, Governor Gooch, for the first time since Boca Chica. Of each, Gooch asked first after the health of their men and grew more visibly distressed as each officer had only a tale of mounting deaths.

It was Captain Washington, commander of marines aboard the Admiral's ship, who brought news of an exchange of correspondence between the Admiral and the General. Vernon had urged Wentworth to bypass San Lazaro and attack the city immediately. The General had demanded 5,000 more troops; apparently he was setting up outposts all over the place as he had at Boca Chica. The

Admiral had refused the additional troops; he thought the General had sufficient forces on land to overwhelm San Lazaro if he would push the attack. He even sent plans for the attack, and reminded Wentworth that a French buccaneer had stormed the fort and charged into the city on the heels of the routed defenders. The letters had been couched in formal terms by the Admiral, but beneath the stiff sentences there was acid anger, and the General, in his equally formal replies, grew more annoyed and nervous with each exchange.

The morning after the visit of the captains 200 Americans, drawn from the *Hampton Court* and neighboring vessels, were sent ashore. Instead of arms they carried scaling ladders made aboard ship, axes for cutting fascines, and bags of grenades which they were to supply to the assaulting British soldiers. They were followed by Jamaicans who also were to be used as a work force.

The Americans found a British regiment occupying an area on the shore that included two small estates and a tiny village of thatched huts. Another regiment had been sent to reconnoiter the approach to San Lazaro and the city, the narrow defile between La Popa and the lagoon where, Greg knew, only four or five men could march abreast on the road. As the Americans approached the hill they heard a volley of musketry from the direction of the defile, followed shortly by another and another, a pause, some more volleys, then silence.

Sometime later Jed learned from a soldier of the Fifteenth Regiment that the troops had been ordered merely to feel out the place, clear it of Spaniards, and then halt. "It made them sick. A good general would have ordered them to follow the Spaniards and keep on blasting them, and would have thrown all his forces behind them at once. They'd have taken the city before night. Now I'm betting we settle down, pitch camp, and make ready for a proper siege according to the rules." He spat in disgust.

That was what happened. Wentworth waited for cannon from the ships, tents, and supplies. He drew up elaborate plans for a battery with a platform, entrenchments, and all the rest to fire on San Lazaro, and he put the Jamaicans to cutting down some woods to make a camp. He had about 1,500 regulars ashore, but he told the Admiral that was not enough, and, giving the Spanish strength as reported by deserters, again demanded the 5,000 troops.

The Admiral, more and more anxious and impatient, must have sent a peremptory reply, or perhaps Wentworth was growing uneasy at the loss of men. The tents the Jamaicans had put up were filled with fevered soldiers unfit for duty. The rest of the troops had been for three days without shelter from the merciless sun or the sudden showers which presaged the rains that were bound to come shortly.

At last Wentworth called a council of his officers. The engineer pointed out the increase of fever among the troops, the imminence of the rainy season, the lack of trained gunners, and urged a surprise night attack on San Lazaro without delay. Otherwise they would have to reboard the ships and return to Jamaica. Brigadier Blakeney opposed the attack, but the majority reluctantly voted for an assault in the early hours of the following morning.

There was nothing to do but wait through most of the night amid the confusion and murmuring stir of hundreds of soldiers trying to get some rest before the battle. Farther away, but within earshot, was the camp of the sick, where stricken men raved in delirium or lay in torpor awaiting death. No fires were allowed, and the dry biscuits that were issued after midnight were so hard they had to be softened from canteens before they could be chewed. From the lagoons came clouds of mosquitoes to settle on any exposed flesh. In spite of orders against noise, the sound of slapping was like the patter of rain.

Greg, Jed, and Sam stayed together. Assigned to them was one ladder, a spade, and two bags of grenades. At two in the morning the regulars formed lines near the landing beach. The plan was to attack both sides of San Lazaro simultaneously. A Colonel Wynyard was to lead the attack with 500 grenadiers on the steeper side of the hill, obliquely facing La Popa, and would be supported by half the Americans with their ladders and grenades. Colonel Grant was to lead the attack on the other and easier slope, the one overlooking Cartagena, with the Fifteenth and Twenty-fourth Regiments and a mixed company drawn from the Thirty-fourth and Thirty-sixth, with some Americans in support. Finally, there was to be a reserve of 500 marines. All this was clearly explained to the attacking soldiers. The assault was to begin at four o'clock when all but the Spanish sentries would be asleep. It must be pressed to success hard and quickly before dawn, because after daylight those storming the northern side of the hill would be under fire from the guns of Cartagena, which could sweep the slope with canister shot.

With fifty men in the lead, followed by the rest of the grenadiers, the Americans, then the regulars, and, last, some marines, the column began to march, feeling its way to the road and along it towards the two hills, through woods and darkness filled with the chirps and croaks and stirrings of unidentifiable creatures of the tropic night. In the small valley between La Popa and San Lazaro fireflies, larger and more luminescent than any Greg had ever seen, flickered constantly, giving the scene a strange and weird light.

Accompanied by two Spanish deserters as guides, the grenadiers turned off the road and began to feel their way to the foot of the slope. Colonel Grant and the regulars kept on the road around the hill, turned inland and realigned for the assault.

Greg, Jed, and Sam kept close behind one company in spite of the weights they carried. The orders were to get up the hill without alarming the garrison, then rush to the wall, plant the ladders, swarm up to the parapet, clear it of the enemy, and kill or take prisoner the garrison. But first there was a wait of nearly half an hour for Colonel Grant's men to get into position.

Then the ascent began. It was slow work and became slower still as the slope steepened. Peering through the gloom, Greg could make out dim figures ahead. Some were digging their boots into the ground and clinging with one hand to rocks or tufts of coarse grass as they struggled upwards. Others were crawling on hands and knees. The silence was broken only by infrequent tiny clanks or rattles.

The troops had not quite surmounted the steepest part of the climb when a Spanish musket above spat a brief flame into the darkness. There were shouts of alarm and more muskets took up the fire. The grenadiers crawled on, panting, struggling up the iron-hard, steep hill. A blast of cannon burst above them. Grapeshot whirred overhead. A grenadier gasped, tried convulsively to rise, lost his hold, and rolled down the slope.

"Steady, men," called an officer calmly. "We're near the top. Get up fast. Take shelter against the wall. Their cannon can't reach us there."

Struggling for breath, with sweat running down their faces in the heavy, humid air, Greg and Jed hauled at the ladder while Sam heaved up his two bags of grenades. All the guns on this side of the fort were now in action, depressed as far as the gunners could lower the muzzles, pouring a deadly rain of canister on the grenadiers. Men were falling, their bodies sliding or tumbling down the hill.

Now they were at the top and running for the shelter of the wall. But suddenly a new obstacle met them—the wide ditch Greg had seen the Spaniards digging. Some men fell into it. Others halted quickly on the brink. An officer rapped out a curt order. The men recovered quickly from the surprise and as quickly formed ranks. Another order and a volley crashed at the Spanish musket men on top of the wall. Officers shouted orders all along the grenadier lines. There followed what seemed a series of complicated evolutions made all the more mysterious by the darkness and the toll the enemy fire was taking. But these troops were disciplined British soldiers, and Greg admired their stolid steadiness, as they filed to left and right around the ends of the uncompleted ditch.

"Lord, I'm going to get me a musket," grated Sam. "There ought to be enough of them around here."

"Not yet," Greg told him. "They may be needing grenades and ladders any minute now. That's our first job."

Most of the grenadiers, still spaced in ranks before the wall, began hurling grenades up at the Spanish on the parapet. Some exploded; many apparently did not. The troops were now protected from the murderous grapeshot of the cannon, but they were still exposed to musket fire, fortunately not very accurate. The fighting had spread to another face of the fort where a company of grenadiers clustered beneath the bastion at the corner.

"Ladders!" called the captain of the company ahead of the three. "Forward ladders!"

Greg and Jed rushed to the sound of his voice and planted the ladder against the wall of the bastion at his direction. Calls rose from other officers, demanding ladders. A few were produced, but nothing like the twenty-five or so which had been assigned to this side of the fort. Greg concluded, with shame, that many of the Americans, denied arms by the British, had flung down their ladders and grenades and retreated when the shooting started.

A sergeant began mounting the ladder they had put in place. Soldiers climbed after him. He reached the top and shouted back, "It's four feet too short." The rattle of fire drowned out his next words, but he must have been given a boost by the man behind him, for other figures followed up the ladder until suddenly it broke in two and dropped the men to the ground.

In the half-gloom which now heralded the swiftly approaching dawn, two more ladders were set against the wall. Under the cover of fire from others who, crouching, shot at the parapet, a file of grenadiers went up one ladder and pushed three men over the top of the wall. Another file started up, but finding the ladder too short descended helplessly to join in the futile firing and hurling of grenades that seemed to be doing little damage, so closely did the troops have to hug the base of the wall to avoid the cannon shots.

Sam had already given his bags of grenades to the British. It was rapidly growing light and Greg ran to find more bags where their bearers had dropped them. Ducking here and there, hiding behind rock ledges when possible, he and Jed recovered several bags of the weapons which the grenadiers at once began to toss over the wall. As they scrambled in their search amid rocks and sprawled red-coated bodies they came across several colonials who had seized muskets from the fallen and were firing at the heads that appeared and disappeared above the gray walls. As night turned into day the Spaniards could aim with more certainty and the toll of the British grew. Greg wondered what had happened to the few grenadiers who had gained the parapet. He hoped some, at least, were prisoners.

"This is no good," said Jed suddenly. "If the regulars haven't carried the other side of the fort—and there's no sign of that—we're licked. We three better get out of it. But," he added grimly, "I'm going to take a crack or two at them before I go."

He crawled down among the rocks to where a dead grenadier lay and gently eased the musket from a flaccid hand, loaded, and primed it. Crouched behind a pile of bodies, he aimed and fired. Bullets from the fort flicked past. Jed reloaded and suddenly rising

to his feet took careful aim and fired again. There was a crash of musketry from the parapet. Jed stood, swayed, and began to crumple. Greg jumped to catch him and felt a blow on his left shoulder.

Sam leaped down beside them as Greg tried to unfasten Jed's coat and shirt. As he fumbled with them blood gushed over his hands. Aghast, he looked at Jed and mumbled, "We'll get you down and away from here, Jed. Don't worry."

The brown eyes looked fixedly at them. Suddenly the weathered face smiled. "Past worrying I am. Got in two shots, anyway. Helps make up for some of our fellows throwing down ladders and running. And I got hit from the front, way it should be, not in the back."

"Don't talk," pleaded Greg. "Sam, let's get him behind that rock so it's between us and the fort, and take him straight down the hill."

Gently they raised him and carefully they began to carry him down the hillside. He had closed his eyes. Once he gave a little groan of pain. When they stopped to rest, beyond the reach of bullets, he opened his eyes. "Know I'm a goner. But bury me in the ground, boys. Don't want to be shark bait. You've been good lads. I'm sorry to be leaving you." The words came in faint gasps.

"Quiet, Jed," soothed Sam. "We'll git you down where we can bind up your wound. We'll take care of you. You'll git well."

In Greg's heart was a numbed sadness, for he feared that Jed was right. They picked him up again and staggered down the slope, carrying him as best they could away from the firing and the carnage. He was still breathing when they reached the road and started for the defile. They stopped again when they had passed it. As they laid Jed down in some shade he put one hand flat on the earth, smiled into the distance and gave a long sigh.

Sam knelt to listen for his heartbeat. "He's gone," he mumbled after a moment and burst into tears. Greg sat down. His throat tightened and his eyes filled. It couldn't be true. Jed, companion, best friend . . .

They took him up, determined to carry him back to camp for a decent burial. Behind them the sounds of useless battle went on as the sun mounted into the brazen sky. From the increased roar it was evident the guns of Cartagena were now turned on the hapless regulars who had tried the other side of the fort. The fight couldn't go on much longer.

The two were nearing camp with their burden when the sounds of battle ended and Sam suddenly sat down. "Can't go farther," he told Greg sheepishly. "Seems like my legs are shaking too much to move. If you can walk to camp and git a spade we'll bury Jed there by that big tree. I can dig, anyway."

As Greg went for the spade he wondered if Sam was getting the fever, for a shaking ague was one of the signs. But, hard as the ground was, Sam managed his share of the digging, though they wished they could have made the grave deeper. Instead, they piled stones on top.

"We ought to say something," ventured Greg from the midst of a great desolation. Sam nodded. So they knelt and said the Lord's Prayer together. At the end Sam added, "He·was a good man, Lord," and neither was ashamed of sobbing.

By the time they reached camp Sam was shaking. Greg put his arm over Sam's shoulder, but Sam jerked away. "What you doing? I can walk now. Look, you got hit yourself! You got blood on you."

Amazed, Greg looked at his left shoulder and remembered the blow he had felt as he caught Jed. It did not seem to hurt. "Got nicked, I guess," he allowed, and put his right arm around Sam's waist. This time Sam did not object. As they entered the camp, where a few marines had been left on guard, Sam said he wanted to lie down in the shade of one of the tents which was filled with fevered men. Greg brought him some water, helped him out of his jacket and made it into a pillow, and sat beside him. There was nothing more he could do at the moment.

Some time later those of the grenadiers and the regiments under Colonel Grant who had survived arrived in camp along with nearly all the contingent of Americans and the marines who had covered the retreat. All were weary and disheartened. The fort of San Lazaro stood intact and unconquered and closed the way to Cartagena. There had been a truce with the Spaniards while they buried their dead, 179 in all, officers, non-coms and soldiers. The wounded, more than 450, were being brought back in some carts previously collected from around La Quinta. Of the more than 1,500 Englishmen who had set out in the night hours of that morning some 650 had been killed or wounded. American losses were slight. But many still fit for duty seemed about to come down with fever.

From those Americans who had been attached to Colonel Grant's force, Greg learned what had happened to their attack. The Spanish guides were soon suspected of having mislead the column to a part of the hill that came quickly under the fire of the fort. Colonel Grant had been mortally wounded by one of the first shots. According to a British soldier who was near him when he fell he had gasped: "The General ought to hang the guides and the King ought to hang the General." The whole army repeated what he had said. It was a fitting comment from a staunch soldier who had been needlessly sacrificed in the bungling that had resulted from the clash between Vernon and Wentworth and from Wentworth's incessant delays.

After the Colonel fell a paralysis had seized the force he had led. Line officers, unaware at first of his death, had waited for his orders. When they found they were leaderless they issued conflicting orders or none at all. The result was that the troops on the north face of the fort never even reached its walls. They fired helplessly at it until daylight when the guns of the city opened on them and reinforcements of Spanish infantry issued from its gates to complete the rout. Now all must wait for the General and his precious council of war to decide what to do next. So many soldiers were down with the fever that at this rate there would soon be no army left.

Greg spent all his time with Sam, who got worse and worse. On the third morning he clutched Greg's hand frantically. "I got the fever. I know. Seen too much of it. Don't let them send me to the hospital ships, Greg. No medicines there, no surgeons, nobody to feed and care for you. I'll have a better chance to throw it off here. Stay with me, Greg. Get me water and I'll git well."

Greg promised. He had fixed up a half shelter from a torn piece of tent and some sticks to keep off the sun and made a gruel out of moldy flour. Even water was hard to come by, and he had to scout around for enough to prepare the mush and to keep Sam's face cool and for him to drink as the fever mounted. Then, later, all he could do was sit and hold Sam's hands as he became delirious. Around them the army lay in misery, awaiting orders.

The fever took its victims quickly. On the fourth day Sam died, smiling because he thought he was in Virginia. Greg and another colonial buried him beside Jed. Afterwards Greg found he had to fight against a profound depression and thought longingly of home.

Then came the first downpour of the rainy season, a drenching cloudburst at noon that continued for an hour and flooded the camp. Thereafter the rain fell regularly each day at the same hour, turning the camp into a steamy slough and making life even more miserable. After three days of this orders came to move the surviving troops back to the ships. The wounded and sick already had been rowed to the hospital ships which, in spite of the death rate, were always overcrowded. By this time there were few Americans on the shore. Greg knew he had been lucky. The bullet of San Lazaro had merely creased his shoulder and the wound was healing. He went to where boats waited for the troops and recognized a sailor from the *Hampton Court*. As he took a seat in that boat he saw a familiar figure coming over the stern. The man turned away his face, but Greg had already recognized Vizer Bates. It seemed to Greg ironical that this man, whom he had not seen during the fight or afterwards, had lived when so many better men had died so horribly. Wearily, he regretted that Bates would be on the same ship, for the man would remind him of Jed, who had so distrusted him. Greg resolved to avoid him.

The relative order on the ship was a relief after the confusion of the army camp. Greg reported to a sergeant then hastened to wash up. Later he was sent for by Governor Gooch. The Governor was sitting in his chair in the shadow of the poop deck, his legs still propped before him. He greeted Greg warmly, evidently relieved to see him whole and well. When he asked what had happened the sound of his familiar voice and the kind expression on his heavy face almost made Greg break down and cry. Sitting on the deck by the chair Greg managed to hold his voice steady as he told of the camp and the battle. When he came to Jed's death he had to stop for a moment. A hand dropped gently on his shoulder and in a bit he continued.

"I am glad you are safely returned," said the Governor at the end. "Keep me company now. We'll be leaving for Jamaica and then, because of these," he gestured at his legs, "I hope to return soon to Virginia."

They waited in the steaming harbor. All day boats and barges from the ships were rowed to shore with bodies to be buried and returned with stores, tents, cannon, all manner of gear, and then went back with their dead. The Governor watched, his face a mask. In spite of orders, the big lagoon began to be littered with useless objects thrown overboard; pieces of plank, empty barrels, straw mattresses whose owners no longer needed them, whatever would float moved languidly on the shining ripples.

Now Greg began to wonder about Mr. Ogden, the emeralds and the schooner from Jamaica. She should be waiting by now at the Bahia de Barbacoas. He was thankful he had fulfilled his mission; the rest was up to that strange man, the merchant.

At last the ships in the bay nearer Boca Chica moved out as the mild breeze filled their sails. Then slowly, in groups, the others stood out from the shore while the guns of Cartagena thudded an ironic, triumphant farewell salute. The *Hampton Court*, in the last group to leave, lingered off Tierra Bomba.

From the deck Greg could look at the misty rise of the hill where he had found *Casa Hermosa* and then around the shore and islands to the inlet he knew was the Paso Caballo, to the tangled mangroves that edged a swamp called Honda, and thence to the mouth of the harbor. There was so much he could never forget. He thought of the assault, of Jed and Sam, of the thousands more who would never see home again, and blamed the mist in his eyes on the sinking sun which was now turning the water into a sheet of unbearable gold. The *Hampton Court* would sail in the morning.

Sleep was fitful that night. On one side of him a Maryland man muttered and tossed; on the other, one from Massachusetts alternated snores and groans as he moved an injured leg. At last Greg rose and went on deck in search of a breeze. No one noticed him as he made his way to the rail and looked again toward the terrible land he was leaving.

To the east the sky lightened; the quick dawn was coming. An object splashed into the water. Wondering what would be thrown over at such an hour, he leaned across the rail to peer down. He did not hear the steps behind him. Suddenly his feet were lifted and he was thrown over the rail. He had just time to close his mouth and hold his breath before he hit the water. He came up quickly and looked up the side of the ship. A figure stood where he had been. In the growing light he could distinguish the man's thin body and reddish hair as he leaned over and looked down. There could be no doubt: it was Vizer Bates. He waved one hand and moved away.

In a flash Greg knew at last who had bribed the Jamaican boy to take him to Quinzaine's house in Kingston. Bates, who had joined the expedition in Williamsburg at the last moment, was a secret agent working for both Quinzaine and Captain Bartlett—and against Mr. Woodford!

Greg trod water and shouted. No one answered. Again he shouted. Above him loomed the towering ship. He swam to the side and touched the slimy planking. There was no hold there. As he bumped along towards the bow a sudden clamor broke out on the decks above. The capstan began to creak as sailors pushed it around: the anchor chain rattled through the hawsehole. Greg shouted, but the noises drowned his voice. Frantically he swam further to catch the anchor as it rose. The anchor broke water; he was almost there. He reached and his hand slipped on mud-coated metal. The anchor rose above his head in a cascade of mud, slime, and water, and he went down in a little whirlpool caused by the suction of the lifted weight.

He came up. The ship was already yards away. He could never reach it. He looked for another, but the next hull he glimpsed was also moving seaward. He began to swim frantically. There might be another ship beyond. In a moment common sense returned to him. He'd wear himself out that way. He must not lose his head. His hand struck a plank. He tried to rest his shoulders on it, but it promptly sank beneath him. He saw he would have to swim alongside it, resting one arm at a time. He stopped, treading water and drawing in his breath in long gasps. He was alive. He must think. As he rested he saw the last of the ships turn in stately retreat to enter the Boca Chica passage.

TEN

To the Schooner Agatha

THE plank was cranky, with a mind of its own and hard to manage, but he had to keep going. But where? Thanks to his view from the ship's deck he knew the Paso Caballo was nearer than the shore below Mr. Ogden's house. And beyond the Paso would be the schooner *Agatha*, his one chance to get back to Jamaica. But first he must reach land. He remembered the tales of sharks in the harbor and thought he saw one triangular fin ahead of him, but told himself that he was imagining things!

After a half hour of swimming and resting Greg saw to one side a sizable object lazily bobbing in the sea. Working his plank toward it, he saw it to be a hatch cover about five feet square, probably from one of the sunken Spanish ships. Pulling himself up onto it, he found it would bear his weight and that by using the plank as a crude rear sweep he could progress across the lagoon. For what seemed a long time he labored, panting and sweating, under a sky filled with a clouded but still brazen sun. He was very thirsty.

Again he thought he saw a shark and splashed violently to scare it away. Next he thought he saw a small boat but decided he was wrong. Then there was another, a dugout canoe, low in the water, with four men paddling. It might be a risk to call them but he must chance it. He lifted the plank and shouted "Help." The dugout altered course.

As it came alongside four impassive faces surveyed Greg. The men seemed to be Spanish Indians, like the herdsmen. Two leaned over and held the hatch cover and helped him into the canoe, then retrieved his plank and laid it in the bottom of the craft, shook their heads at the weight of the cover and let it go. Four pairs of eyes turned again to Greg. His only thought was water. He pointed to his mouth and throat. The man nearest nodded and produced a gourd. Greg gulped the warm liquid thankfully. Another proffered a piece of dried beef which Greg began to chew, now aware he had had no breakfast.

The man in front half turned, grinned and asked a question. Greg had only the two words that had been on his mind these past hours. "Paso Caballo," he said loudly, and repeated it.

"Ah," said the man. "Paso Caballo, si." They all began to talk, apparently discussing what they should do.

While he waited Greg looked over the waters. Three more dugouts were within sight. His own was well filled with salvage from the English and Spanish fleets—planks, empty kegs, pieces of uniforms, rope, a stool, anything that had not sunk was gathered here by desperately poor people who could put this jetsam and flotsam to practical use. The crew hauled in a few more objects while Greg dozed and then, apparently satisfied for the present, headed for the shore. At length pulling the boat up on a shelving bank they began to unload their salvage and nodded approvingly as Greg, wakened, helped them. A waterway, like a small river, lay on their right. The man who had given Greg the piece of beef pointed to it and said "Paso Caballo."

"Bahia de Barbacoas?" Greg inquired.

The man held up two fingers and pointed south along the waterway. Greg hoped that meant two leagues and not two days. The man took his arm and led him up the bank to a group of huts. "Pueblo de Baxera." He waved vaguely, then darted into a hut and appeared with a dilapidated wide-brimmed hat of woven straw in one hand and a chunk of bread and slice of beef in the other. Greg was about to decline the hat, but the man pointed to the steadily darkening sky and spoke so urgently that Greg put it on. This kind person should have some reward, Greg felt. In an outside pocket of his money belt was a shilling. He held it out but the man shook his head and spread his hands, as if saying what he had done was not worth that, but Greg pressed it into the brown calloused hand. The Indian's face broke into a wide grin as his fingers closed over it, he gabbled something, touched his forehead, and trotted to the shore. He ferried Greg across the Paso and showed him the trail.

Suddenly Greg threw his arms wide. He was sore; he had scraped his legs crawling on the hatch cover; his shoulder hurt; he was weary. But he was on land! He started down the trail to the hoped-for *Agatha*.

The track ran parallel to and a little above the Paso, dipping occasionally toward the edge of the mangrove jungle that edged the water or turning into a drier section where low, sharp-edged, cactus-like growths were interspersed with spindly palms. It was a desolate place and he would have liked to hurry through it, but his tired legs made him settle for a steady pace, eating the bread and meat as he walked.

Two Indians passed him, glancing out of the corners of their eyes as they hurried on. The sun was now hidden by dark clouds. Soon came pattering drops of rain and then a roaring downpour that drowned out all other sound and quickly drenched him. He was grateful for the hat sheltering his eyes. After perhaps two hours the rain stopped and the sky cleared. By midafternoon the sun was hot and when Greg saw the bright blue of water ahead his clothes were almost dry. He moved more quickly. This must be the Bahia.

The bay was narrow at the head but broadened gradually until, beyond a far distant point, it widened into the sea. And there, a mile ahead of him, at anchor, pitching and rolling in the sea kicked up by the storm, lay not one vessel but two! Greg stopped. It had not entered his head that the captain of the *Agatha* might not believe his story. Would Mr. Woodford's ring vouch for him? If not, he might have to try the other ship. But what was it doing here?

As he approached the ships he saw that one vessel was schooner rigged, the other a barque. Both were anchored quite near the shore and fairly close to each other. Rope ladders hung down on their landward sides. A boat was putting off from one and heading for a large, palm-thatched shelter above the beach. As he neared it he saw most of the space was devoted to plank tables and benches beneath a roof held up by posts. Faint blue aromatic smoke and the smell of burned grease hung in the still air.

The ship's boat was now touching shore and Greg turned to it. The men, perhaps two Jamaicans and two English, regarded him incuriously. "Has the captain of the *Agatha* come ashore?" Greg asked with, he hoped, adequate composure.

At his words the nearest man smiled. "Thought you might be a guardacosta, with them gaiters and pants," he said. "Captain McKestrick you want? He's still aboard. We're going back for another load. We'll take you, if you like."

On the way they passed a boatload of men from the barque.

The *Agatha* was a two-masted schooner, and, for a ship that carried all sorts of cargo, surprisingly clean, with holystoned deck and shining brass, the kind of craft, Greg thought, that Mr. Woodford *would* own. And Captain McKestrick, waiting on deck, was the kind of captain Mr. Woodford would choose. He was as Scotch as his name, with sandy hair turning gray, a square, sun-and-wind reddened face, and very direct blue eyes.

Greg told his story quickly: he had carried a message from Williamsburg to Mr. Woodford and from him another message to a merchant named Ogden in Cartagena.

"Now, now," clucked the Captain reprovingly.

"But I did," protested Greg. "I'll tell you how later. I expected to see Mr. Ogden here."

"He hasna arrived yet," replied the Captain guardedly. "Continue your narrative."

Early that morning, Greg resumed, as his ship was about to sail, he had—and he hesitated—somehow fallen overboard unnoticed. He had swum around, been picked up by some Indians, set ashore, and here he was. Would there be room for him on board?

"There's room," acknowledged the Captain. "But how should I know it is indeed from Mr. Woodford that you have come?"

"Here," Greg held out his hand. "He gave me his own ring to

wear to prove to Mr. Ogden I was telling the truth. He accepted it."

McKestrick looked at the ring closely. "Aye. I know it. An odd tale you tell, but with this I must believe you. Come. The crew have gone ashore for the evening meal. Let us join them."

As they waited at the rail Greg saw another boat put out from the other ship. "Is that Mr. Woodford's, too?" he asked.

"No. It's the *Turquoise,* out of Kingston, and also waiting for someone or something. 'Tis lucky you came tonight, lad, for when there was no sign of Mr. Ogden after two days waiting I sent a man to his house above the shore. Word came back he would be here shortly after sundown. As soon as we have conducted our business we sail. He will come to the taberna, a fancy name for that hovel."

The Captain steered Greg to a round table with chairs instead of benches. As they were being served stew and baked plantain a large man with black hair and eyes sat down opposite. Captain McKestrick greeted him as Captain Coutts and received a grunt in reply. Apparently the commander of the other ship, he was muscular and bulky of body. Ignoring them, he set about eating large quantities of everything that was served. His name seemed somehow familiar, but Greg could not remember why. Captain McKestrick went on speaking of other matters and Greg forgot the question raised in his mind. From the benches the voices of the crews rose and fell in an indistinguishable babble of sound. Greg noticed that the two crews were keeping to themselves.

It was dark when two horses appeared in the light of the torch fastened to one of the posts of the taberna. The riders dismounted. Mr. Ogden came to the edge of the shelter, leaving the other to hold the bridles. Captain McKestrick rose. "You'll come back wi' the crew," he told Greg, and went to join the merchant. The two moved to a boat on the beach, followed by a sailor who rowed them to the *Agatha.*

Greg had finished. Surely the interview would not take long. He could not sit with the crew, so he left the table and strolled down to the water. In addition to the boats from the ships two small dugouts were pulled up beyond the others. Soon McKestrick's voice came clearly over the water as oarlocks creaked again, "A pleasant journey home, sir."

"And to you a safe voyage," called back the merchant.

Greg moved into deep shadow. For a reason he would have had difficulty naming he had no wish to encounter Mr. Ogden here. Edging along the beach, he looked back at the thatched shelter. Mr. Ogden was sitting at the table with Captain Coutts. Greg turned away and watched the two pinpoints of light rocking gently at the mastheads of the ships. It all seemed odd, and even more odd when two unmistakable figures left the taberna and strode to the water's edge. They pushed a dingy into the water, the merchant settled himself in the stern, the larger man climbed aboard and began to row. Had Mr. Ogden forgotten something on the *Agatha?* But Mr. Ogden was not being rowed to the *Agatha,* he was being taken to the *Turquoise!*

Well, Greg reassured himself, a merchant dealt with many ships and captains; the canny Mr. Ogden must be taking care of two errands at the same time. But why had he waited until Captain McKestrick was on his ship and unable to return? But it was natural Mr. Ogden had not mentioned another errand. Thinking of the interview in Cartagena Greg suddenly saw the face of Walter Quinzaine and heard again the word "emeralds." What would a reputable merchant have to do with such a dubious character, an enemy of Mr. Woodford, and also involving emeralds? And now dealing in secret with this other person. There was no apparent reason why Mr. Woodford should be involved, now, but just in case he was Greg had better find out what was happening. He owed that to his friend. If all was well no one would know.

He eased the dugout canoe into the water, found the paddle, climbed in, and began the sweeping, swirling motion which, noiselessly, without lifting the blade from the water, both propelled and steered the craft. Presumably the whole crew of the *Turquoise* was ashore, but he must be careful lest a guard had been left on board.

The darkness made distances deceptive and he almost ran into the barque before he realized how near he was. He found the dingy and discovered it was tied to one side of the rope ladder, so he tied the frayed painter of the canoe to the other side, and was glad the dugout was moderately steady as he climbed from it to the ladder and up to the rail. The deck was empty and dark except for a square of light from the open door of the captain's cabin in the stern.

There was no sound of a man on guard. Greg took off his shoes and tiptoed to the edge of light, took a hasty look inside, and shrank back into shadows.

He had seen Captain Coutts and Mr. Ogden sitting at a tiny table, glasses and a decanter and what looked like a package wrapped in cloth between them. Now Greg had to depend on his ears.

"If I had known Quinzaine would not be here I would not have come," the merchant was saying in a thoughtful tone.

"He was supposed to come," rumbled the Captain. "When we parted company ten days ago he said he'd meet me here within the week."

"You say he went first to the inlet by Albornos, alone?"

"Right. Said it was easier to operate in and out of Cartagena from there."

"Have you got what he left for me?"

"Yes. Kept it by me." There was a faint clink as if a bag of coins had been thrown on the table. "Seal not broken, you see." The tone was nasty. "You don't have to count it. I'm an honest man, when I'm paid to be. Your seal won't be broken either. Quinzaine will get the packet as it is now."

"I truly hope so, Captain." The merchant's voice sounded oddly smug. "There it is. You are sailing soon?"

"Within the hour. I'm to bear it, full sail, to Kingston, he said, and he'd meet me there if not here."

"Good. I must leave. I don't want McKestrick to know I was out here with you." The merchant sniggered. "His owner is going to be surprised. Quinzaine offered more inducements, and there's nothing like being paid on the spot."

"Glad to help get back at that snotty Woodford, and his captain too. Have another glass before you go."

Greg backed away from the door. The talk about Quinzaine . . . Captain McKestrick's owner would be surprised. It was treacherly—betrayal! The emeralds must be here, on this ship. Then what did Mr. Ogden give to Captain McKestrick? A dummy package? The Captain wouldn't break the seal: the package would reach Mr. Woodford's hands unopened. If it were a dummy Mr. Woodford would be ruined!

The stools scraped as the men rose. Greg darted from the door and crouched in the darkness on the seaward side of the cabin. Would Coutts row the merchant ashore? Was the packet still on the table? If he had to search the cabin the lantern would help.

"I'll go first and steady the dingy," said Coutts.

From around the corner Greg could see the big figure swing over and down while the other waited. A pause. "What's this?" Coutts's voice rose from below. "Did you tell your man to come for you? Is he on board?"

"No." The merchant was surprised. "What's the matter?"

"Somebody's come aboard this ship. There's a dugout tied to the ladder!" Coutts was back at the rail. "Stay here," he growled. "If he comes near grab him. I'll search the ship."

Greg froze. He should have set the dugout adrift! But there was no time for regrets. Bending low, he slipped into the cabin. The packet was on the table. He seized it, opened his shirt, thrust the packet inside, buttoned the neckband, tightened his belt and bounded to the deck like a rabbit.

"There he is," shouted the Captain. "We've got him."

Greg jumped into the darkness and made for the bow. There was no chance of reaching the ladder. He collided with something hard, found it was a rack of belaying pins, grabbed two of them and hurled them across the deck and over the opposite side. The splashes they made diverted the Captain's attention for an instant.

"Did he go overboard, Ogden?" he bawled.

"Don't think so," the other called back. "See no signs."

The Captain cursed and took up the search. Greg crouched at the rail. The Captain was coming nearer. There was nothing to do but swim for it. Greg straddled the rail.

"I see him," cried Coutts. He lunged forward.

Greg drew a breath and dived as a massive hand reached for his shoulder. He came up for air, submerged again, and kicked himself along the side of the ship until he found the anchor chain at the bow. Here he broke surface and listened, clinging to the chain.

The captain was yelling. A pistol cracked into the night. Heavy feet thumped toward the cabin. A moment of silence and Coutts roared, "He's got the packet. We must go after him."

"You can go after him if you like," called back the merchant indifferently. "If he got the packet it's probably at the bottom of the bay by now. And he may be, too."

"But you must help me get it," shouted the other angrily.

"No. I delivered the packet into your hands and I have your receipt for it. I will now go ashore in the dugout your intruder so fortunately left." Ogden's tone sounded amused.

"Ogden, you will give me back that receipt and row me in search of the thief. Quick. There's no time to lose."

"Captain Coutts," Mr. Ogden's voice was firm. "There's no use pointing an empty pistol at me, and without more light it will take you too long to reload. Meanwhile I have you covered. I could hit you without even aiming. Get into your dingy and go about your wild goose chase. I will paddle ashore. Good luck," he added ironically.

The captain cursed but climbed down into the dingy. Greg heard once more the creak of oarlocks and clung more tightly to the slippery links, submerging for as long each time as he could. After rowing around the boat twice in widening circles Coutts changed directions and headed toward the *Agatha*. That was bad. Both crews would be returning soon and Greg had no desire to wait for the men of the *Turquoise*. When the sound of rowing ceased he began swimming toward the schooner. Ten minutes later he was clutching that anchor chain and awaiting developments.

Coutts did not stay long aboard. Greg heard him swearing again as he went down the ladder and cast off. In a few minutes noises rolling across the water from the beach told that the crews were returning to their ships.

Greg waited until the second of the *Agatha*'s boats was alongside. As the last man mounted the ladder and the crew went to the davits to hoist the boat aboard he climbed, dripping, to the deck. Captain McKestrick was standing at the foot of the main mast giving orders. The capstan was manned; the crew sprang to the sheets and the sails rose, flapping until they caught the land breeze and filled. Greg realized with a sense of shock that he had been just in time.

When the schooner was under way the Captain turned his atten-

tion to Greg. "Well, a ducking, eh?" Behind them came a confusion of sounds and shouts from the *Turquoise*.

"A bit of a swim, sir. What's that, from the *Turquoise?*"

"No concern of ours," replied the Captain. "Yon close-mouthed
Coutts runs a taut ship; he'll manage nicely, whatever is wrong. He
paid me a visit, just the noo. Claimed a marauder had been on his
ship who'd jumped overboard. Asked if I'd seen the fellow. I assured him I had not. Nor had I." He glanced at Greg's bare feet.
"He is a hard man, and, no doubt, a complete villain. I want none
of him. But ye'll be wanting your bed. The supercargo's not aboard
so you are welcome to his place." He called to a sailor to fetch a
lantern.

The cabin was just large enough to hold one bunk, with a tiny
space between it and the bulkhead for the hanging of clothing.
Over the bunk was a small porthole. Compared with the transport's
quarters it was luxurious. First Greg looked for a place to hide the
packet and at last saw that one of the inner planks sealing the cabin
was a few inches short in the far corner. There was just room
enough for the packet to be crammed safely in and against the
beam inside.

The first two days were a blur to Greg. Burning with fever one
minute and shaking with chills the next, able only to take broth, he
was afraid he had caught yellow fever. But the Captain was sure
he had merely a touch of the sun, was worn out, and what he
needed was sleep and porridge, plenty of porridge to stick to his
ribs.

And so it proved. On the third day Greg ate his porridge and
fresh beef and ripe bananas and more porridge and thought highly
of the Scots' diet. He asked the Captain if any sails had been
sighted, thinking of the *Turquoise* and its enraged but competent
captain.

"Haven't spoken a one," Captain McKestrick told him. "Each
time I saw one I've changed course. No telling what may be under a
sail. Tell me now of the great expedition and the fighting."

Greg recounted what he had seen and at the end the Captain
shook his head. " 'Tis no wonder we Scots, badly outnumbered as
we are, have been able to hold the English at bay, except now and

then. The Sassenach have the men and the guns, but after the treatment they have given your men from the colonies, and after the plain stupidity they have shown here, I wouldna fight for them and I'm glad I do na have to."

On the fifth day from the Bahia a dark irregular line of land took shape to the north. Jamaica!

"Ye've given us luck, lad," the Captain said. "The wind was right. We've beaten the fleet back. We'll come up to shore this afternoon and lie to 'til morning."

"I can't thank you enough, for everything," Greg began.

But Captain McKestrick cut him short. "Don't speak of it, lad. I'd have taken you aboard even without Mr. Woodford's ring, for I could see you had had a hard time of it. Aye, he'll be pleased to see us both and to learn of what we carry."

Greg fervently hoped that would be true.

E L E V E N

Attack on Bonaventure

IT was past noon when the *Agatha,* having worked her way into the harbor by Port Royal and then across the great bay, approached Mr. Woodford's dock at Kingston. Only transports were anchored off the town. Greg was glad, for he would have time to go to Mr. Woodford before Governor Gooch's ship made harbor. As the *Agatha* was warped to the dock Greg looked back. A small barque was rounding the western point. He wondered if it might be the *Turquoise.* That could mean trouble, but then he decided that Captain Coutts presumably had no way of connecting the *Agatha* with the intruder who had been aboard his vessel for those fateful ten minutes.

"We'll go to Mr. Woodford together, eh?" said Captain McKestrick as he passed Greg at the rail. "But after the siesta hour."

Greg subdued his impatience and agreed. At that, it would be better to present the merchant with both packets at the same time. And wouldn't Captain McKestrick be surprised—as well as Mr. Woodford, if his own suspicions were correct! Under the lightweight sailor's jacket he wore he pressed his right elbow against the bulge inside his shirt, and sat down in the shade to wait.

At first Mr. Woodford's dim office seemed cool, but it was only an illusion due to the change from the glare outside. The Captain and the chief clerk hailed each other decorously but warmly. Mr. Woodford was at the plantation. A touch of the heat, or, the clerk coughed discreetly, perhaps concern over his affairs.

"What has happened?" asked McKestrick quickly.

"There was the loss of the *Nancy*'s cargo, sir, which can never be recovered. Then this office was broken into again, papers disturbed, the safe opened. No great loss, but distressing."

"All the more reason we go to see him immediately," said the Captain. "It is too far to walk. Can you get us donkeys?"

In ten minutes the donkeys arrived, patient little beasts that ambled scarcely faster than a man walked but at least kept the feet off the ground, as the Captain pointed out, even if only by a few inches. The clerk brought them cool orange juice and Greg a woven straw hat against the sun. It was too hot for talk or thought, and Greg dropped behind on the narrow road and found himself dozing to the gentle pace of the donkey.

Sea and clouds were golden as they turned up the driveway of *Bonaventure* and came out at the terrace. From the watchtower a horn blatted. Stanley rushed out the open door, gave a cry of pleasure and called "Mr. Woodford! Come!"

Limping a little, the merchant hurried out. He looked both thinner and more anxious, Greg thought, but as he saw them his face lighted and he laughed delightedly. "The two of you! By all that's wonderful! Welcome! This is the greatest pleasure in months."

The long room was growing dim. Servants hurried in to bring hurricane lamps for the table by the open windows and lighted the candles on the smaller tables. Others brought a decanter and delicate stemmed glasses, and Mr. Woodford filled the three. "The best Madeira," he announced. "Stanley knew I would wish it. It has been saved for a special occasion, and what could be more special? Gentlemen, your health."

Captain McKestrick rose. "Greg, we can't drink to that toast, but we can to one of our own. 'Health and prosperity to our good friend James Woodford.'" He clicked his glass against Greg's and both took a sip. It was a heavy wine, sweet and smooth, and Greg was not surprised it was the cherished drink of the wealthy planters back in Virginia.

As they settled in their chairs servants brought platters of cold meats, hot breads, fruits, and a pot of hot tea to guard against the malaria. Mr. Woodford waved at the plates. "You are hungry, I know. I have waited this long to hear so I can wait a little longer. It is better to talk on a full stomach."

While they ate he talked lightly. He himself was quite recovered and was assured even the limp from his broken leg would disappear in time. There had been a Maroon attack on a plantation toward Castleton up in the mountains; freebooters had raided Port Antonio but had got little for their pains; ships had come from England, but all awaited the return of the fleet to hear of the expedition. Though it was known now that Cartagena had not been taken there might be some compensations for that failure. Greg wondered what compensation there could be for the thousands of sick and dead.

When the table was cleared Mr. Woodford could wait no longer. "You have the stones?" he asked the Captain eagerly.

McKestrick drew a packet from his coat pocket and laid it on the table. "Here they are, sir. Mr. Ogden brought them to me, though a few days later than expected. But lucky that was, else young Shelby here would not be with me."

Mr. Woodford turned to Greg. "I cannot thank you enough," he said quietly. "I was sure you would reach Ogden, if it was in any way possible. My chief concern was for the perils you must have faced, and thankful I am to see you out of them. But where is Jed? I had thought he would be with you."

Greg looked down at the polished table top, striving to control his voice. "He—he was shot—killed at San Lazaro," he managed to say and had to stop.

A strong hand closed over his own. "I am very sorry. He was a good man." The same words, Greg remembered, Jed had used about the merchant. "You must tell me later. Now, how did you reach Ogden?"

Greg recounted the highlights of the adventure quickly and told of the other visitor at Ogden's house and what he had heard and of his discovery of who the merchant's visitor had been.

"Quinzaine!" exclaimed Woodford. "But why—what would be his business? We will talk later, also. Now—the packet!"

From a drawer in the table he took out a small shining dagger and cut the seals and heavy wrapping. Greg almost spoke of his own, but maybe he was wrong. At the thought he winced. If he had been wrong he had turned himself into a thief. The cloth on the table parted to reveal a flat tin box which opened easily. It was full of small objects, each wrapped separately in cloth.

"That is to protect the stones from damaging each other," explained the merchant gaily. He picked up one, tore off the covering and gazed in horror. Instead of the glowing green of an emerald his fingers held a dull rough stone. Frantically he ripped off the other wrappings. Each held a stone or pebble, of no value whatever. "He has cheated me," he gasped.

Greg gave a great sigh. He had not been wrong after all.

Mr. Woodford sat very still, his face white. One hand clenched and unclenched. "I must thank you again for all you have done for me," he said slowly. "But this—this is near disaster."

Greg jumped from his chair. "No, sir. I have another packet. I—I stole it from Captain Coutts's ship." He opened his shirt and drew out the bundle he had carried all day. The size and wrapping were the same as that of the other box. Color came back to the merchant's face.

"How? When? So Coutts was in on this!"

Stammering in eagerness, Greg explained why and how he had obtained the packet. "I owe you an apology," he said to the Captain, who was watching him steadily. "Perhaps I should have told you, trusted you, but after all that had happened how could I be sure I was right? If I was wrong it was better for you not to be involved."

McKestrick nodded. "I was sure you had been Coutts's intruder, and that worried me a bit, laddie. But 'twas right to keep silent. Now let's see what this one holds."

Mr. Woodford's fingers shook a little as he cut the wrappings. Within was another flat tin box with a sheet of paper on top. On the paper was written "To Walter Quinzaine, mcht. of Kingston. Goods as per order. Payment received."

The horn on the watchtower suddenly blatted insistently. The three froze in surprise, turned at the sound of running feet.

Through the wide door into the hall of the house they could see Stanley race to the massive entrance doors, pull them shut and bring down into position the two big oaken beams that barred and strengthened them. "Men coming, sir," he gasped as he hastily shot additional bolts.

"Quick, let us see," gasped the merchant, opening the second box and unwrapping one of the objects in it. It was a worthless pebble, similar to those in the first box!

From the watchtower floated a long, despairing cry.

Stanley whirled. "That's Luke!" and ran for the staircase.

Hastily more stones were uncovered. There was not an emerald among them. The three stared at the two brownish piles.

"It is small comfort that Quinzaine has been gammoned more than I," said Mr. Woodford wearily. "I do not understand."

"But I understand very well, my dear Woodford," said a rasping voice from the long window beyond the end of the table. "Your boy stole my emeralds from my ship, but too late. I have already written to Thomas Spofford of London that only I can supply the gems he ordered from you." His smile as sneering as his voice, Walter Quinzaine stepped over the low sill. He held a pistol in each hand. A mulatto with another pistol followed him. The three waited quietly by the table.

Quinzaine leaned back nonchalantly against the frame of the window. "The *Turquoise* was hard on your heels, McKestrick. They'd have boarded you if they'd found you at sea. However, when I heard the tale today from Captain Coutts, and learned the figure he glimpsed on the ship that night was a boy, I knew where to come to find the stones. It appears that Bates failed in his job of getting rid of him. No matter, now, for we are well met again." He looked around the room. "I'll buy your house from you, Woodford, since you are now bankrupt."

"At least," Mr. Woodford told him with a little smile, though his eyes were hard. "I was not fool enough to pay the full amount for a box of useless stones."

Quinzaine gave a laugh like a whinny. "Stones, yes, green stones. That was how I got them from you. I paid more. Ogden and I concocted the scheme together, though I had thought of it before I went to Cartagena, after I read your papers and knew you would have someone reach Ogden somehow. It would have worked but for him." He flicked an evil glance at Greg. "Call back your man, Woodford, and order him to tell the others not to fight. They haven't a chance. The crew is here. They'd kill the lot."

The merchant shifted his weight, eyeing the man at the window.

"Don't try to jump me," warned Quinzaine. "Together Manuel and I can kill the three of you."

"Quinzaine, you are mad to attack us."

"I am here for the emeralds, and I mean to get them."

"But, man, there are no emeralds in either of the boxes."

"No emeralds? You can't trick me that way."

"We have both been tricked," the merchant told him grimly. "See for yourself." He gestured to the table. His manner seemed to shake the other's confidence a little.

"Stand back," ordered Quinzaine, gesturing with his pistols. "All of you. Back against the wall over there."

The mulatto raised his own pistol. "You hurry."

The three backed slowly across the room. Quinzaine handed his man one of his pistols. "Keep them covered." He moved swiftly to the table where the lamps shone on the gleaming surface, on the gilt handle of the dagger, on the dull tin of the boxes and the heaps of wrapped and unwrapped stones. Quinzaine pawed through the piles frantically, tore open the remaining covers, then lifted a blackly furious face to Woodford. "You've hidden the real stones!"

"We had no time to hide anything," Woodford told him. "As you see, we were in the midst of examining the second box, addressed to you."

"Ogden!" spat the other venomously. "Cheated by that scheming blackguard!"

As if at a signal there arose a great pounding on the barred door and a clamor of voices demanding admittance. "Chop it down," shouted a voice. "Too slow," ordered a mightier voice. "Bring up the powder keg. Tamp it with the woolpacks. I've always wanted to blow up this place." It could only be Captain Coutts.

Greg watched the man by the table. Quinzaine, frowning, looked at them, at the table, at the open window and back at the stones. He moved quickly to the window. "No. Coutts, don't. You can come here."

"We've got to have our bit of fun. Blow on that match, boys, then get back."

Quinzaine sprang through the window, the mulatto followed.

"Down," shouted Mr. Woodford, crouching behind a chair. Greg and the Captain threw themselves on the floor behind another.

There came a sudden shattering explosion and a sheet of flame as the great doors burst open and the stonework of the lintel, the wall beside the door, and the wall between hall and library crashed down together. Flames began to lick the paneling of hall and room. The tinkling of shattered glass from the windows and shades died away. Lamp and candles went out in the rush of air.

Through the blasted front doors and then into the room leaped the Captain of the *Turquoise*, a pistol in each hand. Torches carried by his crew beside and behind him made his figure seem gigantic. "Now we'll see the pretties," he bawled. "Bring them out."

Through the window stepped a shaken Quinzaine. "Coutts," he called across the din, "you're a fool."

"Bring out the emeralds," roared the other.

Quinzaine gestured at the table. "There are the two parcels—one from McKestrick, one from the *Turquoise*. There are no emeralds in either. Ogden cheated us all."

Unnoticed, the three had risen from behind the chairs and edged forward to watch the confrontation.

"You expect me to believe that?" shouted Coutts. He strode to the table, turned over the stones with the muzzles of his pistols. Muttering angrily, his men crowded around him.

"That's too bad for you, Quinzaine," His voice dropped to an evil softness. "You promised me and my men here half the pretty green stones if we came with you and took them from Woodford, eh, boys? We've come. You say they are not here. I don't believe you. Bring them out now, or we have ways to make you."

"I tell you Ogden cheated us all," cried Quinzaine desperately. "You've got to believe me. He cheated us, I say."

The mutterings turned to shouts of anger. "Find the stones!" "Take him!" "We'll make him talk."

The mulatto who had accompanied Quinzaine ran around to the end of the table, his face contorted with rage. When he saw the brown stones he gave an eerie shriek.

Quinzaine, his eyes fixed on Coutts, raised his own weapon. "You'll get no chance to torture me, you pirate," he snarled. The mulatto whirled, knocked up the pistol and fired his own. Quinzaine, with an expression of surprise, sagged slowly to the floor.

"Good," shouted Coutts with glee. "The double-crossing villain would have got me. We'll get the stones from them. And, boys, the house is ours. Take what you want."

From outside in the hall came a rush of feet. For a split instant Coutts turned his head toward the sound. With a great bound Captain McKestrick reached the table and in a single motion seized the dagger Woodford had used and flung it accurately at Coutts's throat. The big man dropped one pistol, clutched the hilt of the dagger, tore it out and threw it across the table. A great gush of blood came from the wound. Coutts fired the other pistol wildly at McKestrick, sank to his knees, strove mightily to rise and toppled face down on the floor.

Greg grabbed a silver candle stick from a table and flung it toward the mob. He saw a glint as Mr. Woodford hurled another. Led by Stanley, guns and knives in hands, a surge of black men poured through the burning doorway shooting and hacking at the attackers. The men Coutts had brought began to retreat toward the windows, some firing their pistols, others trying to beat the newcomers with torches or stab them with knives. The place was an inferno of shouts and shots, shrieks of pain and clash of steel and crackle of burning wood all beneath billows of dark and pungent smoke.

In a few moments it was over. The torches were seized by Woodford's men. The invaders turned from fighting to flight as they became aware that both of their leaders lay stretched on the floor. Under pressure they backed, and on reaching the long windows poured out into the night and vanished, abandoning two wounded comrades.

Mr. Woodford set down the small chair he had been wielding as a weapon. "Thank you—Stanley—all of you," he gasped. "Well done. Now—the fire. . . ." The smoke was increasing.

"Yes, sir," panting, Stanley raised his voice. "You fought men. Now you fight fire. *Fast*."

The men left on a run for pails of water. Stanley rushed around and lit candles and lamps then ordered the torches carried away and doused and new shades brought. Flames were licking at the paneling and running up the draperies at the window. Greg began to pull them down while water was poured against the walls and across the smouldering rugs. The fires were quickly quenched. That end of the room was a water and blood soaked shambles and a pile of stone and debris half filled the hall, but the house was saved.

"Are any of our people hurt?" asked Mr. Woodford as he coughed and mopped his face.

"Luke, in the tower, was killed, sir. Knifed in the back before he could blow the horn again. When I heard his cry I went to see. That is why it took me time to arm and bring the others."

The merchant shook his head regretfully. "He is a loss. I am sorry. Any others?"

"Three got shot," said Stanley, "four, five say they have cuts. But not bad."

"The fire seems out. See to the men. No, wait a moment." He bent over Quinzaine. "He is breathing, though the wound looks serious. The devil watches after his own so he will undoubtedly recover. Take him to one of the back bedrooms upstairs; I'll come see him shortly. Those two sailors can go in the stables." As the men were being carried away he looked down at the body of Coutts. "No doubt about this one," he muttered. "That was an extremely brave and adroit act, Captain."

"Now I've done it I regret the necessity, even though there was no guid in him," was the answer. "But he'd have killed us all. With him leading, your men could not have stood against his, and we three were unarmed. 'Tis lucky I learned knife-throwing from a Frenchman years ago. It's a handy thing to know in a tight place."

The breeze blowing through the front windows and out those at the back had cleared away the smoke, though the harsh smell of burning wood hung in the air. Servants were sweeping up broken glass, pulling away the rugs, hacking at the charred wood.

Stanley reappeared. "The wounded are cared for, sir, except for the man upstairs."

"Good. Tell our people I thank them, and I am proud of them. I will reward them tomorrow. They can stop cleaning up now; the rest can wait. Captain, I suppose you and I had better go see what we can do for Quinzaine."

Lighted by Stanley, the two left and the servants followed. Greg surveyed the room. The paneling could be replaced, and the windows and draperies, the wall between hall and room rebuilt. It would soon look as before. He crossed to the hall and the mass of fallen stonework at one side of the great front door where the force of the explosion had been concentrated. This was the original masonry of the house and by some freak most of the damage seemed to have been on the inside. He moved closer. The lamplight was having an odd effect on the newly exposed stones. One that had been split apart seemed to be a different color within. He picked up one of the candles and held it close to the broken stone. He was right. There was something odd. Encased in what had been a hollowed-out stone was a metal object, an iron box.

Mr. Woodford and the Captain were coming down the stairs. "We got out the bullet," reported the merchant wearily. "It had broken a rib but was lodged in the tissue. He has lost a lot of blood, but will recover, with time and rest. One of my people will look after him."

Greg scarcely heard him. "Come, sir. Look!" he cried.

They came slowly. "More damage?" asked Mr. Woodford indifferently.

"There's a box hidden in that stone."

"It's a trick of the light. You're imagining things, my boy, and no wonder."

The open stone was shoulder height in the outer wall. Greg tried to pull it apart, then to press on either side in the hope of finding a spring. Nothing moved. He held the candle close. "There," he said. "See? There is something."

Mr. Woodford peered closely. "I don't believe it," he breathed. "It couldn't be Greengold's treasure!" He collected himself. "We'll find out. I'll fetch a sledge hammer."

"It's not possible," whispered the Captain, shaking his head. "The tale of Greengold was made up for bairns, like those of the treasures of Drake and Morgan. Few of the Brethren were hoarders."

Greg was trying again to pull the stone apart. "If there is a spring it is rusted," said Mr. Woodford beside him in a voice suddenly alive again. He swung the heavy hammer once, twice, three times with all his might before the stone cracked farther apart to reveal a stout iron box of considerable size. They pried it out of the wall, and it was so heavy it took their combined strength to carry it to the table.

"Quick, Captain, use the crowbar and chisel I brought," cried the merchant. "I am sure my hand would slip."

Eagerly the Captain went to work; and the box was opened.

Inside lay eight leather bags of varying sizes, dried and fragile from age. As Mr. Woodford lifted one it broke, spreading a flood of glorious green stones across the table. The three stared.

"It *is* Greengold's hoard," breathed the merchant in awe. "And to think I never credited the legend!"

Carefully they removed the other bags. Two contained gold coins —doubloons, French Louis d'ors, English sovereigns, and some they could not name. Three others were crammed with emeralds. A fifth held golden ornaments and small gold animals. The last revealed more emeralds, big exquisite gems without a visible flaw.

Mr. Woodford threw up his hands. "I cannot credit it . . ."

"The hand of Fate," declared the Captain solemnly. "It has punished the evildoers and requited the just. Dinna ye see?" His excitement lent more of a burr to his accent. " 'Tis a logical sequence. If you hadna sent our Greg to yon scoundrel in Cartagena; if Greg hadna survived his perils; if he hadna taken the packet from Coutts; if Coutts and that spawn of the deil, Quinzaine, hadna followed us here and blown open the door; if Greg hadna been sharp enough to spot the box, never would the Greengold treasure have been found."

Mr. Woodford gave a great shout of laughter. "Captain, you are right. I am sure the hand of Fate has been at work on our behalf." He sounded young and light-hearted. "I will put these in my own strong box in my bedroom and sleep with loaded pistols beside me."

"How much of all this is yours, sir?" asked the practical Scotsman.

No longer laughing, Mr. Woodford sat down suddenly. "I do not know," he answered thoughtfully. "That aspect had not occurred to me. I must discuss it with Governor Trelawney. Perhaps none of it is mine. . . ." Suddenly he seemed old and tired again. "We will talk more tomorrow. Our heads will be clearer then. No one could think properly after all that, and this." He gestured to the blasted door and the shining heaps of green and gold.

Greg made his way to the room he had shared with Jed. Before he could even say "emeralds" once he was asleep.

TWELVE

A Matter of Law

By mid-morning repairs to the long room were already under way. Mr. Woodford went back to the quarters to distribute presents to those who had helped repulse the invaders the night before and to conduct a burial service for Luke. After making sure Coutts was buried, at some distance from the house, and looking in on Quinzaine, who was both furious and feverish, he came back to the terrace.

"Let us bring down the box," he said abruptly. When they had, he opened it quickly. "I thought about this problem a good deal during a rather sleepless night," he volunteered. "I was trying to remember the laws governing treasure trove."

"What problem?" demanded Captain McKestrick in surprise. "Man, ye have a fortune. Is it guarding of it that worries ye?"

"No. It is whether I actually have a fortune." He smiled wryly at their bemused faces. "If this is declared treasure trove all of it, under British law, belongs to the Crown."

"What is judged 'treasure trove,' sir," asked Greg.

"I believe any treasure, coins, gold, silver and so on, found underground and whose owner cannot be discovered, is considered treasure trove and, under law, the property of the Crown. The custom goes back to early times when the King theoretically owned all the land of the realm and therefore any treasure buried in it."

"But, sir, this was hidden in the wall of your house!"

"The lad is right," interposed the Captain, slapping his thigh in agreement. " 'Tis only just that ye should have what's found in your ain house. Fiddle faddle to the Crown's claim. There's no reason why ye should mention the matter."

"I'm afraid I must, for its protection, and ours. But first we should have a clearer notion of the size of the hoard. And I confess I would like to see the gems again."

Carefully he removed the bags. When the emeralds were piled in one heap they made a mound of green fire glittering from a thousand facets in the sunlight that streamed through the window. With the heap of golden objects and coins they epitomized all the great treasures coveted by man. Never, thought Greg, would he see such wealth again. How could he ever describe this to his parents?

The merchant regarded the heaps with dismay. "I have no idea how to grade these stones for fire and purity or to estimate their value. That will have to be left for London. But at least we can count them and weigh the gold."

The emeralds were of various sizes and shapes, some small enough to have come from rings or pins or earrings, others so large that only a tiara or stomacher, pendant or necklace, would have been fit to hold them. The coins also presented a problem for some were strange and old, from some treasures of ancient times. The golden animals, which the Captain said probably came from Peru and Panama, delighted Greg as he moved them gently with one finger. When they could stop admiring, two copies of the list of coins, gold ornaments, and figures were made, and added to each copy was simply "429 emeralds of various sizes," for it was impossible to describe them. The gold, by the household scales, weighed a little less than a hundred pounds. Jewels and gold represented a veritable king's ransom, pointed out the Captain, and to think it might go to the King who assuredly did not need it!

"We must restore all this to its hiding place now," said Mr. Woodford. "Tomorrow I will go to the Governor. I will need you both as witnesses. Can you delay your return to the *Agatha*, Captain?"

"Aye. For as long as is needed."

"Can anything be done about Mr. Ogden?" asked Greg, eyeing the two boxes of pebbles on a table in a far corner of the room.

The answer was a shrug. "England's writ does not run to New

Granada, as it might have had Vernon succeeded. Ogden is not likely to try to deal with Kingston soon again. And I thought I could trust him! I would like to know why he acted as he did."

The evening was spent in easy talk. Greg told of his adventures, including how he happened to be floating on a hatchcover in the middle of Cartagena harbor.

"Have ye any idea why the man Bates pushed you off the ship?" asked Captain McKestrick.

"Yes, but no proof, sir. I believe he had me taken to Quinzaine's house that first morning in Kingston, and has been working for him and for Captain Bartlett of Williamsburg. But there is no proof."

The next morning, after putting a guard over Quinzaine, the three rode to Kingston. As they rounded the slope of Long Mountain and the harbor spread below them, Greg gave a cry. "The fleet! It's coming in!"

Rounding the western point, tiny in the distance, men-of-war moved slowly into view. The thuds of saluting guns echoed across the water from Port Royal.

"I must find Governor Gooch!" exclaimed Greg.

"Tomorrow will be time enough," counseled the merchant. "He will surely come to Spanish Town with the Admiral and the General. But I ask you to say nothing to him, or anyone else, of the Greengold treasure as yet. There is always the danger of being overheard. And I must first consult with Governor Trelawney in Spanish Town. We shall go there now."

Governor Trelawney readily agreed to walk in the garden with them. As the shadows lengthened and palms rustled overhead, Mr. Woodford told him quickly of the treasure and how it had been found.

His dark eyes alight, the Governor shook his head. "James, I almost can't believe you. I know the tale of Greengold, but I always held it a mere fancy, like other tales of pirate treasure. The fact is, despite Morgan's vast plunder, I know of no treasure of any value that has ever been recovered here. So, you found the hoard as a result of damage done to your house?"

"Yes, except that it was actually found by this young man, of the American regiment."

The Governor glanced at Greg with interest. "Any prisoners?"

"One dead and buried, three wounded, one of those Quinzaine, trader, smuggler and pirate."

"Quinzaine, eh? I have never been able to catch him at his dirty work. This is luck!"

"But, Governor, I would like your advice," went on the merchant. "You see, I am by no means sure whose treasure this is."

"Eh? Ah, yes. A moot point." The Governor paced back and forth a few times. "We have had no precedent here in Jamaica. Under English law—provided there is no known owner—the procedure is to hold a coroner's inquest to decide whether or not such a find is treasure trove, and thus Crown property. If it is not treasure trove I believe it belongs to finder and the owner of the property in equal shares. And it depends whether it was found underground or above."

"Your Honor, this was *deefinitely* found above ground," broke in McKestrick. "That we can swear to."

"Then do not repair the wall where it was hidden until the inquest is held, for the location is important. I will summon the coroner in the morning and arrange the inquest. Whatever the outcome, I must see this hoard myself. And now, gentlemen, will you dine with me? The Admiral does not come until tomorrow so we can be informal."

After dinner the three returned to Kingston. The next morning Greg found Governor Gooch was at the same house as before. The door was opened by Sergeant Simmons, who stared unbelievingly.

"We thought you were lost overboard!"

"I was, but here I am again, and glad to see you, Sergeant."

"I can truly say the same to you. Now we have fourteen men of the company alive and well, at last count."

It was shocking news. It meant that about five out of six of the men of Captain Walker's company who had sailed from Virginia had been killed, died of fever, or were still on hospital ships. And by far the greatest toll had been from fever.

"What an ill-fated, badly-managed expedition it has been," Greg said angrily.

"Yes, it's bad," agreed Simmons grimly. "Bad for those lost and bad for England and America, if you come right down to it. This don't affect very many in the colonies right now. But if England keeps on fumbling this way, looking down on us as if we were dirt after calling on us for help, in time it might make a lot of difference."

Greg remembered the vehement words and outrage of many of the Americans through these past months at their treatment, and nodded.

The Governor was thinner and graver of face; his legs were still stretched before him on footstools. His large eyes looked weary and sad, but they widened in pleased amazement at the sight of his visitor. "Shelby!" he cried, half starting from his chair. "By all that's miraculous! Where did you come from? You were missing and no one knew how. Here, sit down and tell me."

Greg beamed. It was good to be with the Governor again; it was next to being home. "You're very kind, sir."

"Tell me what happened to you. All I can think of is the gallant fellows we left behind in that infernal hole."

After hearing Greg's carefully edited account of his adventures since going overboard the Governor shook his head. "The luck of the gods was with you. I'll not have you push it further. Stay here. No need to return to the regiment. There's so few left we could scarce muster a small battalion and they're scattered between camps and hospitals and ships. The Admiral and Wentworth are barely speaking, and I'll wager each of them will have a different account to tell when they get to London. I do not look forward with pleasure to the dinner Governor Trelawney is giving."

"Kingston is hung with flags and bunting, sir, and the people are parading and cheer when they see soldiers, as if we had brought off a great victory."

"Ah, they do not know or understand. It is just as well—but Vernon is a good man, I think. The defeat wasn't his fault. He tried every way to get Wentworth to act. But the General was timid and stubborn and so brought disaster to our cause and death to so many." He paused, then went on. "I have seen the Admiral. I told him I was no use to anyone in this shape, for my legs will scarcely hold me. Also, it is time I was back in Virginia. He understood. So I am going home, Shelby, and those of you left from the company of poor Walker are going with me. It's little enough I can do for the men. I tried to get the remainder of the Virginia troops sent home also but failed. Only a small brig can be spared, so I could not press the point. Captain Washington thinks so much of the Admiral that he is not anxious to leave, nor are some others, despite, or perhaps because of, the possibility of an operation against Cuba. But we'll soon be sailing."

At the news Greg felt a weight lifted from his spirits. He had not dared to think much of the future and what seemed, inevitably, further soldiering until his enlistment was up. Hoping he did not seem ungrateful, he explained he had to return Mr. Woodford's horse, and would like to visit a few days at the plantation, if there was time.

"There will be," the Governor assured him. "I'll send you word if necessary. Go along, Shelby, but no more adventuring!"

As he passed Sergeant Simmons on the veranda Greg halted. "Whatever happened to Vizer Bates?" he asked casually.

"Died of the fever and buried at sea," said the Sergeant, "and less of a loss than most."

Gregg nodded: it was good to know for sure.

At the plantation the Captain told Greg privately that Mr. Woodford was worried about the inquest the next day, but striving not to show it. "Our puir friend is under a strain," added McKestrick compassionately, "and no wonder, considering his whole future is at stake."

The next afternoon the coroner and his jury, six planters summoned from surrounding estates, and Governor Trelawney himself, arrived in a body at *Bonaventure*.

"I am not here in an official capacity, James," the Governor assured Mr. Woodford quickly. "I am just curious."

The coroner, a wiry, gray-haired little man, seemed rather overwhelmed by his responsibilities and the unusual character of the occasion.

First the three pointed to the box in its place in the broken stone. Then they carried it to the table, where all settled themselves in chairs ranged around. Bustling nervously, the coroner convened the jury and swore in the witnesses. Each of the three testified how the box had been found. Two planters measured the box and the place where it had been, for the record. Then the coroner announced, "We will now examine the contents of this box."

Astonished ejaculations greeted the flashing, glittering cascades of green stones that poured from the bags and the golden heaps of coins and objects.

"Astounding," murmured Governor Trelawney. "Marvelous." Mr. Woodford's face was expressionless. It was agreed to accept his list, also for the record. At length the coroner recovered from his amazement sufficiently to remember his duties.

He bowed to the Governor. "Now, if your Excellency will excuse us, we will ask leave to withdraw to examine and consider the evidence and reach a verdict." Mr. Woodford led them to the dining room across the hall and closed the door.

He had returned to his chair when Stanley hurried into the room. As he saw what was on the table his jaw fell and he stood transfixed. The merchant smiled for the first time. "Yes, Stanley, we have found the Greengold treasure. A surprise, eh?"

"Y—y—yes, sir," stuttered Stanley. Though he still watched the table as though it might dissolve, he managed to recover some of his usual poise. "Mr. Quinzaine ask me to tell you he like to speak to you and Mr. Shelby."

"Very well." Mr. Woodford rose. "Let us see what he wants, Greg. Governor, you and the Captain watch over, and enjoy, the treasure. Stanley, you might order some refreshments for our guests—and bring them in yourself."

Quinzaine's cheeks were flushed and sunken and his eyes moved restlessly around the room. Wincing, he raised himself in his bed.

"Woodford," he burst out. "You have me dead to rights. I'm in your power. You could go to the Governor and lay charges against me and I'd be cooked." He paused. "So I want to make a deal with you." His eyes narrowed slyly. "I know something that's important for you to know, and especially for this boy. If I give you this information will you go easy on me? I'm ruined here, anyway. I just want my freedom."

"I can make you no promises," said Mr. Woodford coolly. "I

have no reason to trust you. If what you have to say is genuinely important I will consider your proposition."

The man in the bed scowled. "I'm in no position to argue. All right—judge for yourself." His voice was sullen but now his eyes did not waver. "It's about the man in Virginia who calls himself Captain Bartlett. Look out for him, both of you. He owes me money and I'm glad to get back at him. He's working to ruin your friend Pollock and the other merchants. He was run out of England and came to Jamaica. That's how I met him. He had to leave here in a hurry."

"And you've been working with him," charged Greg, "and Vizer Bates was for both of you. That's why he pushed me overboard—because you knew I had recognized you in Cartagena."

"You knew too much. I told him what to do. I suppose it's as well he failed." He went on to say that Bartlett, posing as an honest merchant and planter, bought smuggled and stolen goods of every kind and undersold the markets, and did the same with stolen and smuggled slaves. Quinzaine's part had been to run in goods by night into rivers and creeks of Virginia.

"Including my cargo from the brig *Nancy*," said Mr. Woodford.

The other ignored him and went on. "Bartlett's ambition is to get most of the tobacco trade in his hands. He will then advance money to planters in poor years on promissory notes with their land as security. In time, he could foreclose, get a nice number of plantations, resell them to wealthy men coming out from England, skip Virginia for another colony and start all over again. Also, he has long been a professional gambler. He came here under another name some ten years ago, set up as a planter. You remember the Carey scandal, Woodford?"

"It was before my time, but I heard of it."

"Got some young bloods in his debt, took all their money and two plantations. Carey shot himself and this man got away that night. Write a letter to your Pollock, Woodford, and tell him this. And you," he looked at Greg, "when you see Bartlett tell him Mrs. Carey's body was found after he stole her diamonds and threw her overboard; though it was hushed up there's a man who'll swear to that. That'll shake him," he added with satisfaction, and lay back, breathing quickly from the exertion of talking. "I've said my say.

Bad luck to Bartlett. He owes me a considerable sum, in addition to the price of a cargo of prime slaves I ran into Carolina for him. I'll never get my money. I've told you what I can. It's up to you now."

As they went down the stairs Greg asked, "Do you believe him?"

"Yes, in large part," answered Woodford. "The Carey scandal is true enough; the rest is probable. Something must be done about this Captain Bartlett."

Coroner and jury were waiting when they returned to the long room. The coroner arose and bowed. "Your Excellency, Mr. Woodford, gentlemen. It is my duty to announce the verdict." He gave a little cough. Mr. Woodford watched him without expression. "The jury unanimously agrees that the treasure, not being found in the ground, but above it, to wit, in the wall of your own house, cannot be considered treasure trove and the property of the Crown. Therefore, under the law, half of it belongs to the owner of the property and the other half to the finder.

The rigid self-control of the merchant allowed only a slight smile and bow and a murmured, "Thank you, gentlemen, for your time and trouble in coming here."

"But," went on the coroner, "since the young man has said that you all found it together, that last point appears to remain in doubt. Consequently, it is the jury's suggestion that the remaining half be divided among the three of you."

"No," exclaimed Mr. Woodford. "Shelby found it. Half is his."

Greg was aghast. "No, sir," he protested violently. "We all found it. It was evident to all eyes. I just happened to notice it."

"Count me out," put in the Captain.

Governor Trelawney held up one hand. "I think," he said mildly, "that the suggestion of the coroner and the jury should be followed. As His Majesty's representative in this colony, I so order. I appoint Mr. Woodford as executor of the—er—fund. The three of you are to work out the details." He reached over and grasped the merchant's hand. "James, I congratulate you. There is no man on whom I would rather see good fortune descend. And the laying of the Greengold legend, when we can let it be known, should protect you from further harassment here." He was smiling warmly, and with pleasure.

"Congratulations" . . . "and to a good and honest man" . . . "I am glad for you," echoed the planters, crowding around.

After the refreshments, and talk and fascinated speculation, coroner and jury departed. Though pressed, the Governor said, regretfully, he could not stay the night. Before he left Greg saw Mr. Woodford talking with him a few moments and was sure it was about Quinzaine. When they were alone Mr. Woodford sat down quickly. "I still cannot believe it," he told them. "I dared not show before them, for the sake of my reputation as a gentleman and merchant, how important was the matter. But you both know. I can only say again—I am grateful to you."

It was noon the next day when a clerk from the Kingston office brought two letters. One, from the chief clerk, said a sealed note had been delivered at the office by the mate of a Dutch barque from Curaçao on its way to the Hook of Holland. The paper had been given to the mate by the master of a craft out of Cartagena, with payment for its delivery. The destination of the ship was undisclosed.

With an exclamation, Mr. Woodford ripped the seal from the second letter, read it quickly and began to laugh. "My heart is so light I could laugh at anything today. But hark to this, from Ogden.

> Dear Sir:
>
> I am sorry to have involved you in a scheme really aimed at the scoundrel Quinzaine. When he and your messenger arrived simultaneously, both seeking a large number of emeralds, it was obvious to me that the demand had come from some wealthy personage through a London merchant. Quinzaine's plan was to outbid you for the stones and have me deliver you trash instead. He did not know that I had learned, privately, that he had, in outright piracy, seized a vessel and cargo, bound for England, belonging to me. So I took his down payment, which almost compensates me for the loss of my property. I accepted the smaller down payment from you, which I will return, after this business is completed, with goods of equal value.

After the deliveries to Coutts and to your captain, I quickly gathered a collection of emeralds. I trust, sir, that you, as a business man, will understand my subsequent action and agree that one should take advantage of opportunities. With emeralds in hand, why should I not take the profit? So I am setting out for London. In the end, you will lose no monies expended; Quinzaine repays me for his piracy; all is fair and just.

One more matter. Should you encounter Quinzaine, which I consider likely, you may let him know that his forceable detention for questioning in Cartagena, which enabled me to deliver the package to Coutts before Quinzaine could arrive to discover its contents, was due to my influence with the Spanish authorities.

I am, sir, your humble and obedient servant.

C. Ogden

"What he does not know," said Mr. Woodford with a chuckle, "is the name of my London buyer of the jewels. Quinzaine knew, because he had rifled my papers, but he would not have disclosed it. Yes, I know what you would ask, Greg. The Governor has agreed Quinzaine may leave the island, when he has recovered, but he'll be kept under guard until then, and taken to Kingston tomorrow. I must confess I will enjoy showing him this missive."

"The effrontery of that Ogden," cried Captain McKestrick, and joined Greg in a burst of laughter.

Suddenly Mr. Woodford was all action. "We'll beat him to it. Captain, get to Kingston as fast as you can. He is probably entering the Windward Passage between Hispaniola and Cuba by now. What's his rig?"

"I don't know, sir, but most likely a brig. Not many schooners like the *Agatha* in these parts. I think we can outsail him. And it will take him time to find your London jeweler."

"Right. Enlist extra crewmen, including gunners. Add a few guns, but we must run light. Use my credit to the hilt. Can we sail at dawn day after tomorrow?"

"Easily, sir. And a pleasure it will be to outwit that double-crossing scoundrel. I'll see we get to London first."

"Then be off. Stanley will find you a mount."

Greg almost wished he could sail with the Captain again, but was promised he could, any time in the future, when the *Agatha* came to Virginia.

At supper the merchant seemed younger and happier than Greg had ever seen him. No wonder—the turn of fortune had been complete. Greg was still dazed—he could not believe that he himself actually owned a considerable share of the treasure.

With Stanley on guard, the two of them began to wrap the gold and emeralds in soft cloths for their journey. But in a moment Mr. Woodford drew out a letter and a parcel, which he handed to Greg. "These are for Mr. Pollock, who has been a good and faithful associate. The three emeralds will help him now, and into the future. The note explains this to him."

"I'll see he gets them immediately, sir, and I know he will be grateful." Greg poked a gleaming stone gently. "I would be happy if my family could have a small part of my share turned into jewelry. It is not worn much in Virginia, but a few pieces?"

"Of course. Will you trust my expert in London to make up, say, a brooch, earrings, a ring, for your mother? A ring for your father, and one for your sister when she is older? I'll have a few saved for you for the future, too. A ring for you, too?"

"That is what I hoped for, sir. Thank you." He poked the stone again. "I would like to show one to my family," he said slowly. "They will not truly believe and understand if they do not see one of the jewels. Will you mark this one down in my share, sir? I will sew it in my belt for safety. I—I'd just like to keep one."

"And quite right," the merchant agreed briskly. "Fear not, I will see to everything, and the proceeds from what is sold that is yours will be deposited under your name to be drawn on at any time.

"One more thing. I would like you to have a good luck piece, a memento, I saw how you admired the little gold animals. Here is one I hope you will accept. With it come my gratitude and best wishes." He laid down a strange yet appealing animal, with a small head held proudly on a long neck, an oblong body and short legs. Greg could not help smiling at it. "The Captain says it is called a llama in Peru," added Mr. Woodford.

Greg smoothed the piece gently. "A good luck piece indeed, sir, and one this grateful friend will always cherish."

They returned to their wrapping quickly. In a few minutes Greg asked, "Sir, what are your plans after you have disposed of the treasure? I hope you will visit us in Virginia. My family would be most happy to welcome you."

"I thank you," smiled the merchant. "I wish to spend some time with my own family. Then I think I will return here for a while. Captain McKestrick, with his share, can become my business partner, set up his own business, or retire, whichever he desires." His eyes grew thoughtful. "I will keep the plantation for a time, then sell it. When I do I am going to set my faithful people free and give each an allotment to start a trade or a farm, whatever they choose. I have never liked slavery and I am glad I can afford to do this for them.

"And of course I accept your invitation. I will be glad, on my way back from London, to see you, your family and your country.

"There remains the matter of Captain Bartlett. I spoke of him to Governor Trelawney who will investigate and, no doubt, tell your Governor, who will see that justice is done. Now, help me carry the box upstairs."

Leaving his friend and *Bonaventure* was not entirely sad, for Greg was sure he could look forward to a visit within a year at most.

As he rode to Spanish Town he began at last to realize that now his family's cares would be over. It was more than just that there would be no more worry about crops and prices. His father could buy one of the best Virginia plantations, or move to any place or city he wished, do anything he wished. And, come autumn, he himself could go back to college and his friends. What tales he would have to tell—of danger and strange places, of friendships, and sadness and courage. The one thing, he admonished himself cheerfully, he must remember not to talk so much he wearied all around him.

THIRTEEN

Home to Virginia

THE voyage back was favored by good weather and calm seas, so calm that Governor Gooch could practice walking a few steps. The spirits of the fourteen of the Virginia soldiers on board rose daily as their vessel skirted Spanish Cuba and Florida and moved steadily up the coast. On a morning in early September they entered the Chesapeake. The Governor dispatched a rider to Williamsburg to tell of his return and bring back his coach.

This arrived two days later and with it wagons for the remainder of the company, which was just as well, Greg thought, for he doubted if any of them had the strength to walk to the town. Word of their return had spread. As the little cavalcade made its slow way over the dusty roads, knots of people gathered at crossroads and rushed from farmhouses to cheer and greet the Governor.

On the outskirts of Williamsburg members of the Council, headed by Dr. Blair, met them and rode escort the rest of the way. Bonfires were laid on the green and welcoming banners were strung across the streets above the crowds on the walks and along the curbs. From his wagon Greg looked around at the people, the familiar houses, the trees and flowers. He was *home*. He could hardly believe it.

At Market Square the procession halted and Dr. Blair read a welcoming address which only those nearby could hear because of the shouts and the occasional boom from the small cannon, used to fire salutes, that stood beside the magazine. The Governor, aided

by two footmen, descended from his coach and stood during the speech.

When it was finished he bowed to Dr. Blair and to the huzzaing crowd. "I thank you for your welcome," he said in a strong voice when they had quieted. "I am happy to be home. I deeply regret that so many brave fellows are left behind forever. They deserve the thanks of their King and country. My gratitude to Dr. Blair, who has guided you so wisely during my absence. I will resume my duties as soon as possible. God bless you all." As he was half lifted back into the coach some men gave another cheer which all but drowned out the sobs of the women who had lost sons or husbands or brothers on the ill-fated expedition or who pitied the Governor in his evident pain.

Greg climbed down from the wagon. He must find a way to get to Pine Grove as soon as possible. A hand touched his shoulder and the round face of Mr. Pollock was beaming at him. "Greg Shelby! I am happy to see you. I have been so concerned about you ever since news came of the failure of the attack on Cartagena and the many who had died. You must come at once to my house."

"But—but I must see my mother and father," stammered Greg.

"In ten minutes I will send a messenger. They will stay with us, I hope. Do you come now."

Greg was grateful. His companions were surrounded by friends and strangers, all eager to offer supper and a night's lodging in exchange for a tale of their adventures. Mrs. Pollock welcomed him in her fluttering way and at supper insisted he finish all the fish and roast pigeon and berries because he obviously needed to be filled out. When he had convinced her he could eat no more, he and Mr. Pollock went to sit in the clear, lingering twilight of the garden and Greg told of Mr. Woodford and his kindness and troubles, and, then, of the finding of the emeralds. As he finished he brought from his belt the letter and packet and handed them to Mr. Pollock.

Before opening either the merchant said earnestly, "Greg, I am astounded. And deeply distressed. If I had envisioned all the perils you have run I would not have asked you to be my messenger. But it seemed so simple—and I was more beset than I told you. Captain Bartlett was luring away both customers and sources of merchandise. He even robbed my warehouse. And he has continued to prosper, with quite surprisingly low-priced goods he claims come from New York. The cargo Mr. Woodford providentially sent has helped a great deal, but I am still not in the clear."

"Read the letter, sir," suggested Greg happily.

The other tore off the seal and poured over the short note. With an exclamation of astonishment he hastily opened the package, unwrapped each covering and gazed, wide-eyed, at the emeralds. Even in the dimming light they gleamed with green fire. "I have no words." His voice shook. "Mr. Woodford's generosity . . . your help . . . I do not need to fear any longer for my family . . . I must not forget I owe you five pounds . . . my dear wife . . . if ever I can do aught for you. . . ."

For Greg, Mr. Pollock's emotion was reward enough.

The Shelby family arrived two days later. To Greg's anxious eyes his parents looked a little older, a little thinner, but their happiness was so warm and deep they seemed to grow younger as they embraced him. His mother's eyes were full of tears. His father's clasp around his shoulders was strong. "Thank God you have come back to us," he exclaimed. Greg had to answer some of Susan's eager questions, but the rest—the great news—could wait until there was time for a full account.

That evening the Governor's secretary appeared at the Pollocks. The Governor wished them all, the Shelbys and Mr. and Mrs. Pollock, to come to the Palace within the hour. Greg had been wondering how he could manage to say goodby to the Governor before leaving. Governor Gooch must have had the same thought, and was doing it gracefully, as he would.

A liveried servant bowed them into the Governor's library, a handsome, wainscoted room aglow with candlelight. "Greg," called the Governor from his arm chair by the desk, "I am glad to see you. I would have sent for you before this save for a matter which needed my attention. Also, I wished to renew my acquaintance with your parents." He shook hands with all and spoke in praise of Greg's services to him until the Shelbys glowed and the Pollocks beamed proudly.

Then the Governor's manner altered. "We have one bit of unfinished business, and I wished you all here to see it completed. Governor Trelawney told me of Woodford's revelations about the troubles you gentlemen have had with the man who calls himself Captain Bartlett, and Greg gave me more details of that, and other things, during the voyage home. Since my return I have inquired further. I have learned enough. And Governor Trelawney furnished me with certain documents." He turned to his secretary. "Bring in that man," he ordered.

What Captain Bartlett had been counting on from the invitation of the Governor there was no knowing. But his expression quickly changed from an obsequious smile to a scowl as he saw the others. "Why, sir," he began. "You did not mention—"

"No." The Governor was cold and businesslike now. "They are here for a purpose—and I could add to the numbers who should be here." He placed his hand on some papers on the desk. "I have here documents from Governor Trelawney of Jamaica concerning you, Bartlett. Some deal with the Carey matter—Ah! I see the name is familiar. They tell how you cheated young Carey, among others, and robbed him and murdered Mrs. Carey for her diamonds. But that is not all. I have other documents which expose your dealings in Virginia. We do not tolerate cheats, gamblers, or murderers here. If you wish to avoid prosecution you will at once leave this colony forever."

Bartlett's heavy face had grown more flushed with each word. "You can't threaten me this way," he shouted. "If you take it to court I'll scandalize a lot of names."

"Ah. That is why you thought yourself safe. But you are leaving, Bartlett. And don't question my power." The Governor's height seemed to grow as his indignation mounted. "First, you will hand over the deed to that field that belonged to John Shelby."

"He owes me twenty-five pounds."

"Which I will deliver this evening to your store in return for the paper," put in Mr. Pollock with dignity. "It is the least I can do for Mr. Shelby and his son."

Greg nodded assent. He could take care of that later, and the thought made him proud as he touched his father's arm to stop his protest.

"You will also compensate Mr. Pollock for the goods you stole from him," continued the Governor inexorably. "Your men have been identified and the stolen goods listed. Also, here are the names of three others you have robbed. These affairs must be attended to by noon tomorrow. At that time you will be escorted to Yorktown and there held until you are put aboard the first ship for England."

"But I have my rights—a court trial." blustered Bartlett frantically. "I can't go back to England."

"You have forfeited your rights here," stated the Governor flatly. "You will get your rights to a court trial in England, where your original offenses were committed. That will save this colony and Jamaica a deal of trouble. Ashe," he called his secretary, "You are armed? Take two guards with you and see this man to his store. Stay there to make sure my orders concerning repayments are carried out."

"You can't . . ." shouted Bartlett and started forward, fist raised. Two guards rushed into the room, caught his arms, turned him and marched him out the door. The secretary nodded and followed.

"I will go now for the money," said Mr. Pollock. "I—I can't thank you enough, Governor, for what you have done. I hope I may express my gratitude more adequately later."

"No thanks are needed, sir. I am happy to be able to see justice done. Also, it is for the sake of the colony." The Governor bent his head as Mr. Pollock bowed and Mrs. Pollock curtsied and gave bright bewildered smiles around as they left.

"Now we can visit." Governor Gooch settled himself more comfortably into his chair. "It is good to see you again, Shelby, and the charming Mrs. Shelby. Now that good fortune is yours, I hope to see you acquire the plantation of your choice, and, if you desire, return to Williamsburg as a member of the House of Burgesses. We need more of your kind in the governing of this colony. Also, as you know, I have the authority to grant western lands of Virginia to those who will take them up and fulfill the obligations of building and planting. It is fine country to the west, where one can grow other things besides tobacco, and it needs sound development. In spite of your good fortune, you might consider the idea at your leisure."

"But I do not understand, sir," replied John Shelby, a pleased but bewildered smile on his thin face. "You have spoken twice of good fortune. Our good fortune is to have our son back, safe and sound, from dangers almost beyond imagining. That is more than sufficient for us."

Governor Gooch cast a quick glance at Greg. "So. I see. He has not yet told you. Well, I can remedy that, in part, and he will add more later." He rang a bell. "Will you join me in a glass of wine? And the young lady may care for some comfits. I shall take pleasure in telling of your young man here, and how he has served so well his King, Virginia, his Governor, and, incidentally, his family's fortunes." The Governor gave a deep chuckle as he saw Greg blush. "It is a story I am sure you will find of interest."

Epilogue

HISTORIANS have noted that the brief and indecisive War of Jenkins'
Ear was a relatively minor episode amid the greater wars of the eighteenth century. These conflicts involved not only political and dynastic
interests in Europe but, more importantly, they profoundly affected the
fortunes and futures of the colonial empires of three nations: Great
Britain, France and Spain.

Spain had been first on the scene in the new world. For a full century
before England and France established permanent outposts in North
America, the Spanish, though thinly spread over a vast area, had been
exploiting the gold and silver wealth of Peru and Mexico, sending it to
Spain in guarded convoys. From the time of England's Queen Elizabeth,
throughout the remainder of that century and most of the one that followed, English and French adventurers flocked to the lure of these riches.
They captured treasure galleons and raided and sacked the chief ports
where the treasures had been gathered for shipment.

With the end of the War of the Spanish Succession, in the early years
of the eighteenth century, an agreement had been reached by Spain and
England which regulated Britain's trade relationship with the Spanish
colonies in America. The aim of this treaty was to secure the peace and
end the activities of freebooters. But the restrictive terms imposed by
Spain, which severely limited English trade privileges, inevitably encouraged smuggling. In turn, this led to boardings on the high seas by
Spanish guardacostas of suspected foreign vessels.

So, we come to the otherwise obscure master-mariner Robert Jenkins
whose severed ear gave its name to the war. Commanding the trading

ship *Rebecca* bound from Jamaica to London, on April 9, 1731, he had met a Spanish guardacosta whose captain searched the *Rebecca* and plundered it. One of Jenkins' ears was cut off as a warning (he claimed) and the damaged vessel was set adrift. Jenkins reached London where his story aroused momentary sympathy and was soon all but forgotten. It was not until seven years had passed that a turn in politics gave him his chance for fame.

The government of Britain, from the beginning of the reign of George I in 1714 to its end in 1727 and in the early years of George II, had been increasingly dominated by one of the country's greatest statesmen, Robert Walpole, who became Prime Minister in 1721. His administration was based on the avoidance of war abroad, something which had drained the energies of other nations, and financial soundness at home. Prosperity in England had resulted for a time in strong popular backing for Walpole. But continuing friction with Spain over Spanish colonial trade, whipped up by parliamentary opposition led by William Pitt and mercantile interests, was threatening in the late 1730's to undermine Walpole's leadership.

Naval officer Edward Vernon was among those who had felt themselves thwarted by Walpole's maintenance of peace with Spain. During the long period of this ostensible peace, punctuated by frequent clashes with Spanish guardacostas, Vernon had turned his energies to politics. He was elected to Parliament and joined Walpole's opponents. By 1738 this opposition, backed by an increasing clamor for war, had thundered in Parliament and the press against Walpole's policy.

It was then that the obscure Jenkins re-emerged. Coached well by the Opposition, he exhibited his long-cut-off ear and recounted the story of his mistreatment.

The effect on the war hawks of England was instantaneous. The King would not allow Walpole to resign, but the Prime Minister was forced to bow to the demands for action. Vernon boasted in Parliament that he could take Porto Bello in Panama, chief base for the guardacostas, with only six ships. He was appointed Vice-Admiral in charge of operations in the West Indies and in July, 1739, was instructed to destroy Spanish settlements there and to "distress their shipping by every method whatsoever." England's course was set and preparations were made to send a fleet and army to reinforce Vernon's activities. War was declared in October. Vernon and his small fleet arrived at Porto Bello in November, 1739, and succeeded in taking the town.

The news of his triumph was enthusiastically acclaimed in England, and medals were struck in his honor.

With the American colonial troops and the British regiments, which arrived with Admiral Ogle's fleet from England at the turn of the year, Admiral Vernon sailed from Jamaica, in January, 1741, with the largest English force ever to appear in the West Indies up to that time. It was this force which attacked the rich and famous city of Cartagena.